Crooked Lake

Ruth A. Hankins

DEDICATION

To my mother,
Florence May Jamieson,
who gave me books.

Thanks, mom.

ACKNOWLEDGMENTS

No one ever does anything all by themselves. I could not possibly acknowledge in so short a space all of the beings (I include people, dogs, lizards etc.) who helped me along the way. I can, however, give a shout out to a few special cases.

Mike Hankins - husband, chief enabler, spiritual guide, and best friend.

Linda Peckham - teacher, inspiration, fellow author and friend, who encouraged me, and had faith in my writing.

Andrea King Collier - fellow writer, fierce intellect, kindred spirit and friend.

Forward

"Hey Willie! Last one in buys ice cream," the older boy yells. He swings his bicycle over the curb and pumps the pedals hard. He is halfway to the corner before the other boy gets the kick stand up and runs, pushing his bike, after him.

"No fair," screams the boy. "No fair." He really hates it when Kyle calls him Willie. He's named William, after his dad, and prefers to be called Billy.

This is their daily ritual, the race to the swimming hole. For more than a week they've been banned from their favorite spot, the deep water on the east end of the big lake, while the Chandler Chamber of Commerce held their Annual Bass Fishing Contest. They spent most of that week at Kyle's house, playing video games and watching the new flat screen TV Kyle's dad just bought. Finally Henrietta, their housekeeper, got tired of them hanging around and shooed them out. They did wheelies and stunts with their bikes for awhile in the parking lot next to the Methodist Church. Until the church secretary said she's call the cops if they didn't stop raising dust clouds and scattering gravel. Will's dad's a county deputy so they skeedaddled. The Bass contest ended yesterday so today they're for the swimming hole. Good thing too, it's only morning and already it's really hot and muggy. Neither boy can wait to cool off in the water.

Kyle is coasting and looking back. Billy stops running to get on his bike, and then starts pedaling hard. Kyle lets him get close then slips the bike into a lower gear, leans into the handlebars, and speeds off. "Loser!" he yells back.

Billy pedals as hard as he can but knows he'll never catch Kyle and his new mountain bike. Twenty-one speeds! It wasn't even his birthday. Kyle always gets what he wants. He's the only kid in sixth grade that's got a cell phone. Kyle says his dad is trying to make up for him not having a mother. Kyle's mother left him when he was a baby, just up and ran away. But his dad owns the car dealership in Chandler and does a lot of other business, so he can afford to buy Kyle anything he wants. Kyle even says his dad is going to let him pick out any car on the lot when he turns sixteen.

Billy had a sudden growth spurt this spring. He's nearly a head taller than Kyle. It's mostly his legs that got longer, but long legs don't make a difference when the other guy has a mountain bike. Nobody else in Cascade has a mountain bike. By the time they pass the shoreline diner Billy is breathing hard and can feel sweat dripping down his neck. Kyle stops at the top of Hunter's Ridge and waves. Billy knows it will be like this all the way to the swimming hole. Kyle will show off at every opportunity. It isn't even the winning that Kyle likes so much, it's watching Billy lose.

"He's a jerk, just like his old man," That's what Will Sr. said this morning while they ate pancakes and sausages together at the Shoreline. Being a deputy sheriff makes him kind of hard on everybody. Even himself. "Find someone else to hang around with, Billy," he says. But there isn't anybody else. Not really. And Billy and Kyle have a lot in common. Billy's mother died when he was just a kid. And Will Campion works every bit as hard as Kyle's dad. He just doesn't make as much money. The Campion's don't have a housekeeper like Kyle and their house in Cascade is nothing like the big house Kyle lives in, in Chandler, but Billy can see they're a lot alike anyway.

At the top of the ridge Billy sees his chance. He jumps the shoulder and heads the bike straight down the bumpy hillside. He comes out on the gravel access road and can see Kyle turning into it from Crooked Lake Road just ahead. Kyle doesn't see him yet. He stands on the pedals and his legs are wobbly but he pumps hard. He can't help yelling "Ha!" when he finally catches up.

For a moment Kyle looks startled and pedals harder. Then a mean smile spreads over his freckled face, and for a minute Billy can see how much Kyle looks like his dad.

"Think you're smart huh?" Kyle yells. He sits back on the dumb little seat of the mountain bike, and pushes out one leg out to kick the front tire of Billy's bike. Billy tumbles, ass-over-teacups, into the underbrush. Kyle stands up on the pedals and races toward the opening in the trail, and on to the swimming hole, not even looking back.

"Cheat!" Billy spits as he tries to separate the bike from his torn pants leg. There's a good size gash on his forehead where he caught the handlebar as he fell. A couple of spokes are broken but the bike looks okay. He smears the blood on the handlebar with his hand and hauls the bike upright. His knees are weakish and he leans on the bike to push it back out to the path. His hands are scratched from the dry bushes. He knows his dad's gonna be mad because his pants are ripped, and his knee stings where the bike chain scraped it. He sits on the seat and pulls back the slash in his pants to see the bloody scrape. It's not too bad. He'd got worse when Kyle dared him to walk across the Chandler Lock a couple weeks ago. They didn't know about the accident then. A boater trying to hurry through before the gate was all the way down did a lot of damage to the lock. But they didn't know that then. At least Billy didn't. The gash on his head is bleeding. He uses his shirttail to wipe it away and walks his bike to the clearing. Kyle's bike is in the weeds where he threw it, and his shirt and wristwatch are tossed nearby. Billy bangs out his kickstand and settles his front tire in the sand. He's pulling his stained shirt over his head when he hears Kyle, on the other side of the trees.

"Mackinaw Island Fudge!" Kyle screams.

Billy watches Kyle swing out over the water and let go just before the knotted rope begins it's swing backward. Waving his arms and kicking out his legs, Kyle makes himself a lumpy X shape as he falls to the water.

"Drop dead!" Billy hollers back and thinks, "If he thinks I'm buying him ice cream, after the crap he pulled, he's got another think comin". That's what Billy's dad always says, "Got another think comin." Billy leaves his shirt on the handlebars of the bike and walks through the trees to the edge of the bank. He catches the swinging rope and uses it to lean out and look down into the lake. The water's down, maybe a couple of feet. For a moment Billy remembers the lock, guesses the repairs must have lowered the lake level. Then he looks at Kyle, who is floating all callywampus on the surface of the water.

"What are you doin'?" Billy yells down at him, wondering how he can float like that. Kyle's cell phone, clipped to his belt loop bobbles on the water. Billy almost smiles when he imagines the trouble Kyle's gonna be in. Then he see's the shadowy rectangle in the water under Kyle. Something about Kyle's hands, a looseness, seems wrong. Billy stands on the edge of the bank, staring down, wanting Kyle to stop messing around when a dark purple circle in the water begins to grow outward from Kyle's head.

"Kyle!" Billy screams, scrambling down the mass of tree roots and loose rocks to the water. The rope burns his hand, but he hardly notices. "Kyle!

1

Sometimes an angler catches a fish that's too small, or the wrong sort, and he wants to throw it back, but the hook sets so deep he can't get it out, so he cuts the line and the fish swims off with the hook still in its mouth. Well, that's Crooked Lake for me. I am the fish, and Crooked Lake is the hook, caught in the fleshy muscle of my subconscious. I broke the line the summer I turned eleven. Broke it good too, But I guess I knew that hook would always be there, tugging, trying to drag old memories to the surface. So when Helen calls and says, "Molly, can you do something for me?" I have a sort of premonition; the hook begins to twist.

Helen is my mother, though I have seldom called her that. I am alternately "Molly Dear" or "Damn it Molly" depending on Helen's mood.

"What is it Helen?" I ask, holding the refrigerator door open with my knee while a I wrestle a box of leftover take-out chicken from inside.

"Well, it's just that. . . are you busy next week.? I mean could you do something for me?"

I'm a writer. Helen doesn't consider that real work. She says I'm always home when she calls, so it's not like I have a "real" job. And she's half right, of course. I barely scrape by on freelance projects for the local non-profits. If it wasn't for the trust fund, I'd still be living with Helen.

"What do you want, Helen?" I put the box on the counter and reach for a plate from the dish rack in the sink.

"Well, I mean, I'd do it myself, you know. But I'm so busy right now, what with the auxiliary being audited and the treasurer being so new. I'm sure I don't know how that woman got herself elected. I'm not altogether sure she can count. And then Audrey Johnson is out with shingles, of all things, and I'm knee deep in the annual blood drive with no help what-so-ever. I can't possibly get away. You're not busy are you?"

Helen is reeling me in, like she always does. Tossing out a line of her various good works and then drawing me in with little reminders of my misspent life, She'll wonder if I'm seeing anyone, mention my wardrobe, my biological clock, and tell me about her friends with grand children. I lay the phone on the counter and let her ramble while I open the take-out box and place two pieces of chicken on the plate. Helen hasn't asked for anything since the fiasco with the nursing home holiday party. Has hardly spoken, really. Not that I blame her. But how was I supposed to know that the "Hollywood Revue" I booked for her, was a male strip routine? Well, maybe I do owe her this one. I put the plate in the microwave, set the timer, pick up the phone, close my eyes and sigh.

"Okay, what do you want me to do, Helen?"

"Well, remember I told you the rentals on the old cottage were down? The realtor blames the economy, not that I'm entirely on board with that. But anyway, someone's made an offer to buy the old place, and I'm thinking maybe it's time to sell it. There's some confusion about the deed, I guess. It's all gobbledygook to me. The realtor, Yvonne something-or-other, is in Chandler. She keeps calling, telling me what a good offer it is, and how I should "git while the gitten's good." But I don't know, it's not like I'm ever going to use the place myself, you know, but it's all I have left of my family."

I take the unintended insult and remind myself that she's mostly right. I am more friend than daughter. Just sixteen when

I was conceived, Helen was abandoned, first by my father, and then by her teenage friends and all but the closest family. Family that has been a long time gone.

"It would be such a help, Molly. And you're so clever about things, just like Cliff. I think that's why he did the trusts the way he did. He knew you'd know what to do."

Of course she'd remind me of my obligations to my stepfather. I was four when we met Cliff, a professor at the college where Helen worked. He was already married, not that that mattered. Helen and Cliff were like magnets, instantly attracted and totally captivated. They married the very day Cliff's divorce was final and we three became a family. It was a glorious time. Cliff was like the father neither of us had ever had, and we laughed and smiled all the time. That is until Cliff collapsed and died from an aneurysm in the middle of a lecture on Nineteenth Century Transcendentalism. Helen retreated to her photo albums and a plethora of good works, while I, the eleven year-old de facto trustee of the Swain Family Trusts, reluctantly grew up.

"Apparently it's something we can't do over the phone." Helen whines. "Someone actually has to go there."

It finally hits me. "You want me to go to Crooked Lake?"

"Oh, could you?" The microwave timer goes off, sending a shiver though my body. I am being thrust into a horror novel. A bad one I wrote myself. Where was Cliff when I needed him?

It's probably Cliff's fault I'm a writer. What else does a confused trust fund kid do? In the 20 years since he left us, the only success I have managed was to finish High School. I remember Helen wore a picture of Cliff in a tiny silver frame on her coat lapel to the graduation. By that time she was no longer reduced to tears at the mention of his name. But when I was eleven, and we were newly orphaned, she teetered dangerously on the edge of sanity. She cried while she packed the car and then cried all the way to Gran's cottage on Crooked Lake. It was the first time in seven years we'd gone to the family reunion without Cliff, and it was the worst summer of my life. It wasn't Helen's fault, of course. It never is. I can't believe she's asking me to do this.

"You want me to go to Crooked Lake?" I am no longer hungry. I put the chicken back in the take out box and drop the plate into the sink.

We never went back to Crooked Lake after that awful summer, the first summer without Cliff, the summer that Uncle Ed died. Gran lived on in the cottage, care-taking for some of the summer families on the big lake. But with Uncle Ed gone her spirit withered. She took to drinking and died of pneumonia the following year. Helen blames herself, it's no wonder she doesn't want to go.

"Would you?" Helen whines.

She's my mother. The novel I have been trying to write for the last eight years isn't even close to a good excuse, so I am driving nearly 200 miles north to a place I have spent twenty years trying to forget.

I have a lot of time on the drive up 127 to remember the Crooked Lake of my childhood. There are actually two lakes, Big and Little Crooked. Big Crooked is connected to the Inland Waterway by a lock in Chandler.It is separated from Little Crooked by a small finger of land, too narrow to build even a small cottage on. The wooded land bridge was thick with undergrowth when I was eleven, except where fishermen had cleared paths to the deep water and shaded banks on the big lake side. The same trees that shaded those fishermen in the early morning provided tangled jungle gyms for the local boys at mid-day, and thick ropes were routinely tied to the strongest branches allowing ariel thrill rides that ended in the cool depths of the swimming hole.

I stop at a rest area just north of the Houghton Lake exit, eat the cold chicken I brought with me and drink vending machine orange soda in my car. According to my map, 127 merges with I75 somewhere north of here and then in an hour or so, I'll be turning off onto M31. I look out the window at the cars hauling campers and boats and jet skis parked all around me. A family is posing for a picture in front of their camper. Making memories. Ah, memories.

Somewhere, under the mossy leaf-strewn ground between the Crooked lakes, at the bottom of a deep hole between two ancient oak trees, is a box. An ordinary metal box, the kind that fancy candies used to come in, though what this box contains is anything but sweet. I know it's there because I'm the one who put it there. Where no one would ever find it. Where no one would even think to look. Don't get me wrong. Crooked Lake is probably a pleasant enough kind of place. Pleasant enough, I suppose, if you are just passing by. If you don't have memories like mine. If you don't know about the murder.

2

I feel the tug of the hook the moment I turn onto old Route 31. Indian River is more populated than I remember, and just past Alanson road construction crews have closed off one lane. I am stopped with several other cars while they let the opposing traffic though. Beach chairs strapped across the roof of the station wagon in front of me, a shambles of faded stripes and metal spokes, reminds me of the spindly cots in gran's three room cottage. A wave of nausea hits me, like that last moment when the elevator pauses, just before it settles and the doors open. I glance quickly at the rear view mirror and see my suitcase and computer bag, secured by a seat belt, taking up a mere third of the back seat. Summers at the lake always meant crowded car rides, back seats filled with sweating shirt-tail cousins or neighbor children, the wet of their swimsuits soaking through their towel togas to make dark circles on the upholstery and the dry clothes of their non-swimming companions. For a moment I see myself, a child of seven or eight, squeezed between two noisy, wet cousins, feeling the dark spots growing on my jeans. My shoulders are pitched forward, elbows nearly meeting behind the beefy hands playing patty-cake across me, my eyes focused on the frayed edge of the beach towel near my knee. I am trying desperately to blend into the humid blur.

I shift uncomfortably in my seat, try to be interested in the worker directing traffic, try to remember happier memories.

Cliff and I used to walk around the lake, stopping to talk to men fishing off their docks, women with toddlers splashing near the shore, even waving at older kids on tubes and floats father out. Cliff was a natural talker and just being with him made everything better. Without him I wouldn't wave, I wouldn't even look. The deep water on the Big Crooked side of the land bridge always fascinated me, and Cliff would recite Thoreau as we walked under the overhanging trees that reflected in the surface of the water, camouflaging the gnarled roots that clung to the shore and the fish swimming near the surface. Unlike other places on the lake, where sandy bottoms, visible in clear water, extended for twenty or thirty feet, the drop off here was immediate, and seemingly bottomless. Beyond the land bridge the little cabins of the Shoreline Resort and the gravel parking lot of the Shoreline Diner signaled the walk was ending. We would stop then at the diner, have ice cream with chocolate sprinkles in a glass bowl and talk about whatever book I was reading at the time. It was a welcome escape from the Evers Family Zoo.

But, packed in like hens in a market crate, crushed together in cots and on air mattresses covering pretty much every spare inch of the tiny frame cottage, you couldn't altogether avoid family at Gran's. Nights were the worst, of course, with this aunt or that cousin getting up in the night and stumbling over everyone else to get to the bathroom. And then there were the various sounds of nasal conditions, from Gran's aged wheeze to Uncle Ed's thundering snore. The crickets and night birds were all but drowned out.

And that was Gran's idea of family. She kept the family together by commanding them to congregate for two weeks every summer at the cottage on Crooked Lake. Gran's idea of family togetherness was not mine, and at eleven I was pretty sure that the arthritis that had gnarled up Gran's hands so she could no longer sew, had twisted up something in her brain as well. It was as if she was afraid that too much time apart would weaken the thread that held the family together, so she was always finding ways to shorten, if not thicken that thread.

It's not like I loathed my relatives, except Uncle Ed, of course. Uncle Ed was mean. Most of the "summer cousins" were distant relatives Gran attached herself to. I don't even remember their names. Then there was my cousin Fred. His mother married Helen's brother Frank. He could balance spoons on the end of his nose and he made funny faces just to make me laugh. Sometimes we splashed in the shallows, chasing minnow and frogs. But most of the time I spent at Crooked Lake, I spent reading. The last week of that summer when I turned eleven, I had read Giants in the Earth, cover to cover, four times wishing desperately that Cliff would appear and talk to me. Cousin Fred walked with me around the lake, but we didn't have money for ice cream and sprinkles at the Shoreline, and it just wasn't the same. When the noise and bustle in the cottage would get too much for me, I would take the little fishing pole from the stack in the corner of the utility room, fill a can with dirt and sit and read for hours at the end of the dock while I pretended to fish.

I remember clearly a day, twenty years ago when I sat in the boat with the chaos in the cottage behind me, took off my shoes and stuffed my socks into the toes. The sun baked pleasantly into my back and I gave myself over to the rhythm of the boat as it rocked gently against the dock. Helen and Ed sat on the screen porch and their voices carried over the water like a bad phonograph.

"Sure is a strange one, that kid of yours," uncle Ed was saying. "Don't play with the other kids, , , always got her nose in a book . . .she's starin' off in space like a shitheel retard."

"Shut up Ed" My mother's voice trembled.

The screen door squawked and I could hear the shuffle of Gran's slippers and the tinkle of ice cubes in glass. "Poor child," Gran said. "What a shame she never catches nothin'. Ain't for lack of tryin,' that's a fact." I could imagine Gran's sad face staring at my backside perched on the edge of the rowboat.

"She's slow," Ed said. "Got bad genes, I reckon. That shitheel knocked you up a retard, Helen?"

"Oh shut up!" My mother's voice shuddered across the water, and then her flip flops spanked the the porch boards and the screen door slammed.

"Now look what you've done," Gran said.

And Uncle Ed said, "What? What did I do?"

Again the slam of the screen door. And then it was just the squeaking of the old metal glider and I knew Uncle Ed was still there watching me. I felt a little guilty about my deception, just a little. I sat there, rocking with the boat, listing to the water lap against the sides, reading. I could feel Uncle Ed's eyes following the line from my fishing pole, as it dangled uselessly in the water, the naked hook glinting up at me. Pretty soon the indistinct noises from the house mixed with the sounds of the water and my own heartbeat, like a disjointed lullaby. I kicked the water with my bare feet and splashed some into the boat. Then I stiffened, remembered that I was "fishing," and looked quickly back at the house. No one was left on the screen porch to see, so I kicked the water again. Then I studied my wet feet, dangling just above the water. The texture of my socks was imprinted, like phantom socks, up to my ankles. There was a wide circle of loose skin on my heel, where a blister had broken. The shoes Helen bought me at the beginning of summer were already too tight.

I wiggled my liberated feet and tapped the water gently with my big toe. The circle it created became two circles and then three and kept building until I could no longer see them. I imagined myself swimming flawlessly through the water, gliding like a racing boat or graceful mermaid, escaping. And then, like it always did, reality butted in. I remembered I couldn't swim. My imaginary stroke slipped out of sync, and the water wrinkled up in front of my imperfect stroke. Bunched up like the skin on boiled milk, it trapped me and I struggled to break free. I shook my head to clear away the image then noticed a small sunfish circling my empty hook. "No," I whispered at the fish. "No." It swam away.

I looked down the shore where kids were splashing in the water. It was true, I couldn't swim. I managed a crooked kind of dog paddle. All the cousins could swim, even the little ones. Maybe I was slow, retarded like Uncle Ed said. Maybe it was inherited. What was a shitheel, anyway? My thoughts built on each other like the circles in the water, getting bigger and bigger even as they ran away. I felt very small and exposed. Hunkering down on the uneven boat bottom, I could see only its shell-like ribs and the cloudless sky above. The heckling thoughts disappeared. There was no need to swim, I was alone in the world. I stowed the useless fishing pole, let "Giants" fall to the bottom of the boat, let my head rest on an old float cushion and began to hum a mantra Cliff had taught me. "Om, mani, padme, ommmmmm." The curved sides of the boat returned the chant to me, softened and dreamlike. I closed my eyes and screened out everything else, until all I could hear was my own voice and the gentle lapping of water. The sun baked into my unprotected skin and the boat rocked gently, drugging me into a deep sleep.

A hard rocking of the boat woke me. I was no longer alone. Uncle Ed sat in the back of the boat with oars in his hands and a bottle of beer between his knees. He laughed as he leaned from side to side, rocking the boat crazily. I sat up too and hugged the side, my knuckles white as I gripped the edge, unable to speak.

"Bout time you learned to swim ain't it Molly?"

I looked over Ed's bulk and was shocked to see the dock a miserably long way away. I looked at Uncle Ed, wondered how many beers he'd had, before the one between his knees. There was mocking delight in his eyes.

"Go ahead, Molly-girl, dive in."

Icicles raced down my back. I looked frantically at the cottage, a tiny toy cottage in the distance, but no one was sitting on the glider. No one was standing on the dock. "No," I blurted.

"You can do it, you little shitheel. Hell, I'll bet you swim all the time back there at that fancy city school of yours," Uncle Ed laughed. "Molly-girl, even the babies can swim."

I squinched myself into the bow of the boat and sat numb, hoping for one of those relatives I avoided so much to come out on the porch, and make Uncle Ed row me back. But I guess they were so used to ignoring me that they just went about their business without noticing us. He rocked the boat again, harder. I closed my eyes, wishing he would stop, wishing I was anywhere but in this boat with my crazy Uncle Ed. The rocking slowed and then I felt rough hands pick me up. I opened my eyes to see his terrible grinning face, turned away from his foul breath, as he threw me over the side.

'Got your wish, stupid', I thought to myself as I hit the water, went under and frantically pawed my way to the surface.

"Swim, Molly-girl. I'll race you back."

Gasping and crying, I managed to stay afloat, just barely keeping even with Uncle Ed, who was rowing sloppily back to the dock. I grabbed handfuls of water and swallowed cold gulps of the lake while I tried to scream. I gave up screaming and tried to concentrate on my dog paddle to stay afloat. Something brushed against my leg and I kicked out and reached down into the water. I went under for a moment and scrambled furiously to come back up, only to see the boat getting further and further away. Uncle Ed wasn't even looking back.

I was treading water, instinctively pumping my legs, reaching out with my arms and pulling at the wavelets around me. 'He'll be sorry.' I thought. 'When they drag my limp body out of the water and pronounce me dead. He'll be sorry all right, and Helen will be mad. He'll be really sorry then.' I pictured Helen plunging a knife in Uncle Ed's chest and screaming, "You killed my baby!" And then I quit kicking and let my hands go limp. I held my breath as I sank below the water thinking, "It serves him right."

It was cold, but not unpleasant. I felt the water moving gently around me. When I opened my eyes it was dark, but not inky. A tiny leaf floated past my eyes. And then my foot touched sand. I stood there toeing the cold sand on the bottom of the lake for a moment before I realized what it meant. I'd passed the drop off and there were only thirty some feet of shallows between me and the cottage. I bent my knees and pushed myself back to the surface where I kicked and grasped at the slippery water until I could feel the sandy bottom with my feet while my head remained above the water. I was still a long way from the cottage. I walked in a few paces and stood in the water watching Ed maneuver the boat and tie it to the dock. If I didn't go in, Uncle Ed would think I'd drowned. And he'd have to tell Helen what he'd done. So I stayed in the water.

And I stayed there even when Helen came out and called for me, and I heard Ed tell her I probably just wandered off. For a moment Helen's head turned in my direction, and I thought she might see me. But she turned and walked off toward the neighboring cabins. I stayed in the water till they turned on the lights, till my toes went numb and I was shivering. Then something brushed against my leg again and I forgot all about Uncle Ed and crashed noisily through the dark water to emerge, teeth chattering and covered with goose bumps just as Gran opened the screen door and hollered "Christ -a-mighty!"

Helen quickly wrapped me in a towel and hustled me into the cottage. After a hot bath and towel buffing, I was put to bed in Gran's featherbed with a hot water bottle and a healthy drubbing of vapor rub. I wasn't sorry to miss supper. Gran made hot dogs again.

"What was she doing?" I heard Gran ask.

"I don't know, mother. I don't know." Helen's voice trailed off into sniffling.

"Shitheel," I heard Uncle Ed mumble.

I only pretended to be asleep when Helen came back and tucked the blanket up around me, though I was so exhausted I could barely move. She touched the wrinkled tips of my fingers gently and I felt her hot tears as she kissed my forehead.

"I love you, Mother," I managed to whisper, as she closed the door, in a voice so small that only the crickets, warming up for their nightly concert under the floorboards could hear me. Between the rough sheets, with the comforting water bottle at my feet, and a door between me and the snoring cousins, I imagined a dozen horrible ways for Uncle Ed to die.

3

I hear a car honking and look up. The road construction guy is waving me through. He's turned his sign to the side that reads "SLOW," and is gesturing at me to move. The car behind me honks again. I put my car in gear and swing out into the open lane. We snake along the ruptured road for almost two miles, and when we pass the lone flag man at the further end, the car behind me speeds up and passes. The children in the back seat make faces through the window as it speeds away.

Nothing in this landscape looks familiar to me. I expected to remember landmarks, and my state map is useless. I'm pretty sure Crooked Lake Road runs off 31, but I'm not sure exactly where. I pass a billboard that announces a new development, called North Shore, on Crooked Lake and lists a realtor in Chandler. Another four or five miles and I turn onto Crooked Lake Road. I'm surprised to find it is paved, though not recently. Pot holes filled with temporary patch make effective speed bumps. I check the speedometer and slow the car. Now the landscape begins to look more familiar. The roller-coaster two-lane winds and dips through the trees, teasing me with short glimpses of lake through the branches. I have a moment of panic, feel a sharp jab like a hook in my throat, remembering where it is I am headed. Just when I think I have the situation under control, convince myself the past was just some freakish movie plot, and not the real world at all, I get snagged on some innocent circumstance, something totally unrelated, and it yanks me kicking and screaming clean out of the water.

The boy is just sitting there, in the middle of the road. I slam on the brakes and stop, straddling the centerline. I have trouble unlatching my seat belt, and forget to scan the area for disreputables before getting out of the car. A hasty look around after I reach him reveals only trees and the dusty shoulder of the road. I haven't seen another car since I turned onto this road, The boy's knuckles and arms are scraped and bloody and his bare chest is oddly stained. Under the stains and a summer tan, his skin is pale and pocked with goosebumps. I'm reminded of the flaws revealed by a sculptor in raw marble, before sanding and polishing soften their edges. When I reach out to touch him, I am not surprised that he is cold. He will not look at me.

"Are you all right?" I ask, knowing full well he is not. He shudders. I want to wrap my arms around him and comfort him but I cannot. I am not good with children. Not even with perfectly normal children, and this one is clearly not. I fumble in my purse for the cell phone, dial 9-1-1, looking up and down the road hoping another car will suddenly appear. The phone rings. Thank God they have emergency dispatch.

"9-1-1, what is your emergency?"

"Yes! Hello. There's been an accident, I think! This child, a boy, he's sitting in the road and he's bleeding."

"What is your name, ma'am?"

"Molly, Molly Swain. I'm not from around here."

"What is your location?"

"I, um. . ." I turn to look around me. A gravel road angles off just past my parked car. "Well, I'm not exactly sure. I know I'm on Crooked Lake Road, I turned off 31 about five minutes ago. There's a gravel road here, goes off toward the lake I think."

"Did you hit him ?"

"What?"

"Did you hit the boy with your car?"

"No! Good grief, no! What are you trying to say? Just get someone out here, this kid's hurt!"

"We have units rolling. Is the boy conscious? Is he responsive?"

"He's conscious, but he won't talk or look at me."

"Has he lost a lot of blood?"

I look at the scratches on his arms. "No. I don't think so. But he's pretty banged up. And he's wet." Just then the boy begins to shake. I take off my linen jacket and wrap it around him. He's still shaking. I sit down on the road beside him and put my free arm around his shoulders. He looks up and I see a gash on his forehead.

"Wet?" the operator asks.

"Oh, God, he's got a big cut on his forehead, it's bleeding."

"So he's wet and he's bleeding?"

What, is she deaf? "Yes!" I yell into the phone. "He's got a big cut that's bleeding and he's soaking wet! Like he took a shower with his clothes on, wet. Maybe he was swimming." Suddenly the boy leans into me, hard. His arms hang loosely by his sides, his upturned palms raw and red, his shoulders like shovels in my chest. I wrap both arms around him to keep from tipping over. His wet hair smells like lake water, reminds me of summertime. I find myself whispering in his ear. "It's all right. I've called for an ambulance. Someone's coming. They're sending someone. Everything's going to be all right."

"Ma'am?" It's the dispatch operator. I let go with one arm and hold the phone to my ear.

"Ma'am?"

"Yes, I'm here." I begin rocking back and forth, holding the boy. He quiets a little, but does not stop shaking. I can hear a siren in the distance.

"They should be arriving any minute, ma'am. I'm going to stay on the line until they get there, all right?"

"Whatever," I say dropping the phone and wrapping both arms around the boy. We rock together and I listen to the siren getting louder and louder. The boy's shivers are intermittent now and he's almost stopped crying. Whatever happened to him, it must have been awful. I think back to Uncle Ed's swimming lesson and being wrapped in warm towels and Helen holding me tight and rocking me while she hummed and cried. I hug the boy tighter, put my cheek against his head and begin to sort of sing/hum the only song I can think of. "Country Roads, take me home, mmmmm mmmmm mmmm mmm . . ."

The paramedics are unloading their gear when the patrol car comes up from the opposite direction. The officer leaves the lights flashing and walks toward us. Suddenly he is running and he falls to his knees next to us, and stares hard at the boy.

"Will. Billy, what happened?"

"Do you know him?" I ask.

"He's my son," the officer says, his eyes never leaving the boy. "Billy, tell me what happened."

"Hey Campion." the paramedic arrives, sets his gear down and says, "I need some room here."

Reluctantly the officer stands and looks away. He sniffs loudly, then stands with one hand on his belt buckle and the other on his holster, and coughs. The paramedics begin examining the boy and talking into a radio. I loosen my hold so they can get a blood pressure cuff on the boy's arm but he reaches out and wraps his arms around my neck, knocking my hair clip loose. I feel tendrils of hair escaping the clip. I feel his rapid heartbeat against my shoulder and the urgency in his vice-like grip.

"It's okay, Billy. These people are here to help you. I'll be right here, I promise." I pull his arms away but keep holding them as I stand up. "I'll be right here, okay?"

"Are you his mother?" the paramedic asks pulling Billy's arms away from me.

"No," I say quickly. "No. I found him here. I'm the one that called it in." I remember my cell phone and look to see the second medic picking it up and talking to the dispatcher. Then he hands the phone to me and I try to wrestle my hair back into the clip as I watch them work.

"It's Billy, my son," the police officer says, stepping forward. "

"Billy? My lord, he's practically a grown man? Has it been that long? Seems like it was yesterday Laurie was bringin' him round to the station in a stroller."

"Almost 7 years," Officer Campion says a little roughly.

"Sorry, Will. He's got a gash on his head, some kind of blunt trauma. Hands are scraped or burned maybe? These wounds on his arms and legs are superficial. Pupils are dilated and his pulse is rapid. Pretty hard to tell if he's concussed or in shock. I don't think it's too serious, Will, but we'll be taking him in to Chandler Memorial. Is this a crime scene?"

"A what?" Will Campion asks.

"A crime scene. Awful lot of blood here. See that pink on his jeans, and the staining on his chest. That's blood. Diluted, but blood. Head wounds bleed a lot, but he's just covered in it. More than that cut on his head accounts for. My guess is there's another victim around here somewhere. One that's bleeding pretty bad."

"Oh Christ!" Will says under his breath. "Miss, did you see another boy? There was another boy with my son."

I shake my head. The officer looks wildly around. "They'd have been riding bikes. Where is his bike? Billy, where is your bike?"

The paramedic swabs the boy's head wound. Billy closes his eyes and tears squeeze under his eyelids and run down his face.

"We need to find the bikes," the officer says to me. "There's another boy might be hurt."

"We?" I say. "I just, I mean, I'm not even from around here."

"The other boy might be hurt too," he says. "We need to find him. Where, where would. . ."

"Swimming? I ask.

Will Campion looks at me. "What?"

"Swimming," I repeat. "He's wet, so maybe he was swimming."

"Oh, God," Will Campion says, running toward the gravel road. "If he's drowned . . ."

'That wouldn't explain the blood,' I think as I follow him down the gravel road. I recognize the land bridge as we approach it. The trees are bigger, and the path wider, but I can see the waters of Little Crooked through the trees to my right and I know that the big lake is just through the trees on my left. I get a chill feeling as I run between them, wondering which tree hides my box of secrets.

"Sweet Jesus," Will Campion is saying as he stands on the bank. Before I can get past the trees, he turns back and yells. "Go get the paramedics. I found the other boy."

I turn and run back through the trees to the roadway. The boy, Billy, is on a stretcher and they are loading him in an ambulance. "Wait!" I yell. "There's another boy!"

4

It's been almost an hour and the ambulance is just now closing it's doors. The boy they pulled from the lake looked pretty bad. They worked on him a long time before they loaded him in the back. The road is crowded with emergency response vehicles. More than enough equipment for a drowning, I would think. I see at least three county patrol cars and two fire trucks. A state police command car is blocking the road behind my car. I've been asked to wait, but they seem to have forgotten about me. So I'm just sitting in my car in the middle of the road. I've checked for voice mail messages, and plugged my cell phone into the charger. Now I'm just waiting. The ambulance finally pulls out, lights flashing, siren pulsing. "Hang in there boys," I say quietly to the passing vehicle.

Officer Campion is watching the ambulance too. I can't see his face but his body language is all defeat. He still has one hand on the holster, but the other hand is raised to his chest. His shoulders sag forward and he looks like an inflatable doll with the air leaking out. As he turns to watch the ambulance roll away I catch his attention. The bewildered, lost look in his eyes turns into a scowl.

I stand and yell over the car roof. "Can I go now?"

He shakes his head.

"I'm only going as far as Chandler," I explain, grabbing my purse and closing the car door. He's walking away as I approach, and I talk while running. "I have an appointment."

"Nobody leaves until we sort this out," he says tightly, not even turning around.

I block his way and try to reason. "But I don't have anything to do with any of this. I just found the boy, sitting there in the road. Look, here's my card. My cell phone number is right here. I'm tired and hungry and I just want to get back to my own life, okay?"

"Nobody leaves" he snarls, looking briefly at my card and then shoving it in his breast pocket.

A black SUV pulls in where the ambulance pulled out and another ambulance pulls in behind it. The SUV driver motions to the ambulance crew and they turn off the flashing lights and remain in the cab. Office Campion clears his throat and hurries over to the SUV. I return to my car, turn the key on and flip through the local radio stations. There is blood on the back of my hand from the boy. I find a tissue in my purse and dab at the stain. Then I notice the front of my blouse is dirty and wet. What little I can see of my face in the rear view mirror is smudged too. I check my hair, it is sticking out at odd angles from the hair clip like a wild brown cyclone. I take out the clip, brush my hair with my fingers and then wind it in a loose twist before putting the clip back. Okay, but not great. Then I look in the back seat for my jacket. My jacket, damn, it must have gone in the ambulance with the boy. I push myself back in the car seat and stare out the windshield.

A huge crane lumbers into the throng of police cruisers and fire engines. Then an old flatbed truck follows. A couple of county deputies, each carrying a boy's bicycle, emerge from the trees and a state trooper directs the crane and the flatbed down the narrow gravel path toward the lake. I try to imagine what they might need a crane for, and how they will manage it given the terrain. I reach for my purse on the passenger seat. I think I might have a roll of breath mints in it.

"Miss Swain?"

I jerk, grab the steering wheel and drop my purse. I can hear the contents rolling on the car floor.

"I'm sorry. I didn't mean to frighten you. Are you Molly Swain?" It's the SUV driver, a huge bear of a man.

"Yes," I say , as I retrieve my purse and look up at the man's face. "I'm Molly Swain."

"My God! It is you!" the man exclaims, pulling open the car door.

I look carefully at his face as I get out of the car. His features are generous. Ruddy cheeks, a bulbous nose, a receding hairline. St. Nicholas, I think to myself.

"Don't recognize me, eh?" He laughs. "Maybe if I hung a spoon off my nose. . ." He pushes the tip of his nose with his forefinger and crosses his eyes.

"Freddie?" I gasp. "Cousin Fred?"

"At your service! My god, Molly. What's it been twenty years? Guess I've changed a bit, eh?"

"Cousin Fred." I shake my head. Why should the cheerful face of my cousin Fred pull on the snag in my throat. "I can't believe it," I choke.

"So, what brings you back to the Lake? I hear you're a writer. Anything I might have read?"

"Probably not," I tell him and then I smile, remembering the joke books and science experiments Freddie used to bring to Gran's cottage each summer.

"So, okay. Are you married? Can't tell by names anymore. Lots'a women keep their maiden names when they marry now. Not my Carol, of course. But then her maiden name was Schnechenburger. Evers is much easier to write. So are you?

Married I mean. Got kids? Dogs? Coming back to live in the old homestead?"

"God, no," I say. Then looking at his hurt expression I laugh nervously and add. "No time for a husband, or kids, though I almost had a dog, once. Congratulations, for Carol. You have kids?"

"Two," he says proudly pulling out his billfold and flipping through the plastic pockets to school pictures of two tow headed children. "Girls. Given names are Frieda and Charlene, but they go by Freddy and Charlie. Couple of real keepers."

"They're beautiful," I tell him. And they really are, although they look nothing like Fred. I imagine Fred's wife to be a stunning blond Viking.

"They're wait'n on ya, Evers," the state trooper hollers from the cruiser behind us.

"Tell 'em to keep their shirts on," Fred hollers back. "Keepers" he repeats in a lower voice, folding the wallet back into his back pocket. "I gotta go to work now. Come on, we can catch up on old times." We cross the road and walk along side the deep ruts the crane has made in the ground and I wonder what job it is that Fred has to do.

"It's great to see you Molly. Carol is going to love meeting you. I've told her lots of "Lake" stories. We have a place over on the big lake now. Oh you'd know it, the old Stephenson place. 'Course we fixed it up a bit. So, what've you got to do with all this?"

"Nothing," I assure him. "I'm on my way to Chandler, to do some business for Helen. I just happened to be the one who found the boy and called it in. Now they won't let me leave."

"Well, that's routine, considering the situation."

"What situation? And why are you here, Fred?"

"Me, well I'm the M-E."

"The what?"

"County Medical Examiner. Forensic pathologist, really. Of course I'm also the assistant fire chief of the Chandler Volunteer Fire Department, and Mayor Pro-tem while Chuck Bauer is out havin' prostate surgery. Small community, I wear a lot of hats."

We near the place where the boy drowned as the crane is being maneuvered into position. Several low branches are ripped off by the crane's wide body as it angles between two large trees. Heavy anchoring pods extend from the main body crushing the undergrowth and scraping the tree trunks.

"Jesus, Campion!" Fred yells as we approach several men standing on the bank. "You're destroying the scene. Is this really necessary?"

Will Campion turns and raises his hands palms up in a gesture of helplessness. "Better see for yourself " he says, stepping over the tree roots and making a place for Fred along the bank.

"Campion," Fred says nodding his head toward me, "This is my cousin Molly. She's a writer. Molly, this is Deputy Will Campion."

"We've met." We both say at the same time. I smile, thinking of the old child's game Fred and I used to play. Pinch, Poke, owe me a coke. Campion manages a grimace.

"What the hell is that?" Fred bellows looking down the bank.

"Diver says it's a 1964 Mustang Coupe."

"Got a plate?"

"Yeah."

"And?"

Campion checks a small notebook he pulls from his breast pocket. "HBC 742, 1964 Mustang Coupe, registered to Robert Matthews of Chandler, reported stolen January 10th, 1997."

"The car Charlene stole?"

"Looks like it. And it gets worse."

"Thought it might."

"Diver says there's two bodies in it."

"Shit!" Fred says, banging his hand into the tree trunk beside him.

5

"Who was Charlene?" I ask Carol as she shows me where to put my bags. For a moment Fred's wife is perfectly still, suspended in a moment of time, like a deer caught in the headlights. The she bends to straighten an imaginary wrinkle in the bedspread and manages a tight smile. The old Stephenson place has never looked better, an old three story Victorian painted white with dark green shutters with a wide verandah facing the lake and a large porch and new two car garage off the back. Fred won't hear of me staying anywhere else. He say's the rustic cabins at the Shoreline haven't aged very well, though the diner is still the best place, next to his wife's kitchen, for a home cooked meal. The bathroom where I freshen up has an old fashioned claw foot tub, set beneath the sloping wallpapered ceiling of a gable alcove. The mirror above the pedestal sink is set in an ornate picture frame, painted bright yellow to match the tiny flowers on the wallpaper. I bend my knees to center my reflection in the frame and adjust my hair clip.

The room they've prepared for me is large and friendly and furnished in a collage of mismatched antiques. Carol opens the window and leans back to show me the view. It's like something out of a travel brochure, green lawn, sandy beach, wide expanse of blue green lake. The sun is almost at the tree line across the lake, making the tips of the trees glow and painting a golden walkway across the water. I can almost see the land bridge between the lakes directly across, and when I lean out, I see the Evers L-shaped dock extending out onto the lake on the nearer side. Fred and Officer Campion are standing near a rowboat and a pontoon boat moored to the dock.

"Originally we planned to open a bed and breakfast," Fred's wife is saying. I duck my head back into the room. "But after the girls were born Fred decided he didn't want a bunch of strangers coming and going."

"It's really nice," I tell her. "Thank you for letting me stay."

"Oh, I didn't mean you." Carol's face turns a complimentary shade of pink as she maneuvers a small sliding screen into the open window. "You're family. And I've always wanted to meet you. Fred is always telling these fantastic stories about Gramma Evers and his crazy family. You'll meet the girls tomorrow. They're staying with my mother tonight, it's our anniversary. Would you like a cup of tea?"

"Oh, I am intruding! I'm so sorry."

"No, it's okay. Fred's job is always interfering with our plans. It's better that the girls are away from this right now, but I hate being alone. It will be nice to have some company while Fred's working."

"Well, if you're sure I'm not a bother. I could really use a cup of coffee," I say and we start down the ornate wooden staircase to the kitchen.

"Who was Charlene?" I ask again.

Carol stops for a moment, then walks stiffly and when we reach the bottom of the stairs she turns toward me and I see the tears in her eyes. "Charlene was my best friend," she says.

"I'm so sorry," I say. And then we are silent as she moves about the kitchen spooning instant coffee into large pottery mugs, pouring hot water from a large tea pot on low on a back burner, and bringing spoons and a small pitcher of milk to the table. Finally, as she spoons sugar into her own mug she sighs heavily and says, "Charlene was my best friend. We went all through school together." She lays the spoon on the table and picks up her mug, then continues. "We played summer baseball together, even had our ears pierced together the summer we turned sixteen." Carol reaches up and unconsciously fingers the small pearl stud on her ear. "And then she married Bobbie Matthews. She went missing when I was pregnant for Charlie, our youngest."

I can hear Officer Campion's patrol car turning onto the road and as Carol and I sip our coffee we can hear Fred coming in through the front door. He makes himself a cup of coffee and sits with us at the table.

"So, you all settled in Molly? What do you think of the place?"

"It's beautiful Fred. Thank you for letting me stay."

"Glad to have you. It's like a flash from the past, seeing you. Makes me feel like I'm eleven again, huntin' morels, catchin' frogs. I'm gonna be pretty tied up for a while with this mess the boys found. . . "

"Is Kyle going to make it?" Carol asks, then suddenly she grasps Fred's hand and asks, "Does Bobby know?"

I can tell from the way Fred looks at his coffee when he answers, that he cannot lie to this woman. "Too early to tell," he says. "Bobby's with Kyle now."

"Not that, you know what I mean. Does Bobby know they've found Charlene?" She is staring daggers at her husband, and although he is not raising his eyes, he is wincing from the blows.

"No." he says." He's got enough on his plate with Kyle right now. They'll tell him about the boy's accident is all."

"Where it happened?"

"Yeah, I guess."

"Then he'll know, won't he?" she challenges, standing up from the table and setting her mug down hard. "He'll know that you found Charlene, won't he? Because he's the one that killed her and put her there, you know."

"Carol," Fred says, finally looking up into her eyes. "You don't know that. And we don't know for sure if it is Charlene."

"But it is the Mustang, isn't it? Charlene's Mustang?"

Fred shrugs his shoulders and looks down at his hands.

Carol looks at me and says, "Ask him what Charlene told us. Go ahead, ask him. In this very kitchen the night before she disappeared. Ask him!" Then she runs crying from the room.

Fred leans back in his chair and closes his eyes. We sit quietly and sip our coffee. The sun drops below the treeline and shadows crawl across the room. The yard light stutters on and throws a square of yellow through the window and across the table between us.

"Want to talk about it?" I ask.

"No," Fred says, and we sit in gathering darkness until the house is quiet and the only sounds are the crickets outside and a low motor out on the lake. Fred leans forward and crosses his arms on the table. In a very low voice, almost a whisper, he says "Do you remember the time when we found the dog in that spring trap up on Hunter's Ridge?"

"The one Uncle Ed killed? Yeah, how could I forget? "

"Put out of its misery, he said. Too far gone to be helped."

"Uncle Ed was a horrible man. I hated him for killing that dog," I said without thinking.

"Did you?" Fred leaned back, making his chair creak, and coughed. "I've been wondering, you know, how he knew. I mean, how do you know when it's time to put a beast out of its misery?"

6

I wish Fred hadn't reminded me about the dog. Even the friendly warmth of my cousin's guest room can't keep me from shivering as I remember. I sink into the soft bedclothes as a ribbon of unwelcome videotape unwinds in my head.

We had climbed the wooded hillside, that day, to Hunter's Ridge.

"It's dead," Fred said, walking a wide circle around the dog.

"It's not either," I told him.

It was a yellowish sort of animal, with long ratty hair and its leg caught in a trap.

"Poor dog," I said. "Poor dog. I won't hurt you." The dog let me touch his head. Fred pried the teeth edges of the trap apart and I pulled the dog's bloody foot, carefully, out. Dried blood smeared my hands, the dog whimpered.

Fred said the dog was too weak to move so we decided to go back to the cottage for food and water. Gran caught Fred in the kitchen. He told her we wanted to have a picnic with a friend up on the Ridge. Maybe Gran was relieved that we were, at last, making friends, anyway she made peanut butter sandwiches and filled an empty milk jug with lemonade for our picnic.

Sam, that's what I called the dog. Sam had peanut butter sandwiches and lemonade for three days, and I stole some mercurochrome and rags from Gran's bathroom to clean the wounds. We took turns sitting with Sam, up on Hunter's Ridge. I didn't see Uncle Ed till it was too late.

"What'cha got there, Molly-girl?" he said stomping into the clearing.

I didn't say anything. I just sat there with Sam's head in my lap and a half eaten sandwich in my hand.

"It's a dog," I heard cousin Fred say. He walked around Uncle Ed and stood next to me, with his arms folded across his chest.

"You sure?" Uncle Ed laughed. "Poor excuse for a dog if you ask me."

"Nobody asked you," I snarled.

"Well, aren't you a little shitheel," Uncle Fred said. "You know they eat dogs some places."

"Not this dog," I told him, leaning over to shield Sam. "Nobody's eatin' my dog."

"Well, no, nobody'd want to eat that crappy sack of shit. Probably got mange and scurvy and distemper to boot. Kindest thing to do for that dog is put it out of its misery. Nothin' that pitiful should be allowed to live. Helen know about this - dog - Molly-girl?"

I hated Uncle Ed. He was the one with mange and scurvy and whatever that other thing was. He shrugged and walked down the hill. Fred and I stayed with Sam until dinner. We decided to tell Fred's mother about Sam. Aunt Harriet liked animals. If Uncle Ed told Helen - and I was sure he would - she'd make us take Sam to the pound.

After dinner, Gran made us dry the dishes, so it was getting dark by the time Fred and I got back up the ridge. Sam didn't whimper when we called out to him, and when we reached the clearing we saw why. The matted hair between his eyes was dark and sticky. Fred said "He's been shot!"

I ran all the way to Gran's cottage where Uncle Ed was cleaning his pistol at the kitchen table.

The raw remembering chills me . The videotape stutters behind my eyes.

I remember standing, shaking, at the screen door and listening while he told Helen and Gran that some old stray dog got caught in a trap up on the ridge, and he had to put it out of its misery.

Cliff's old yoga chant spills from my lips as I pull up the bed covers and turn out the light. "Om, mani, padme, Om." I hold the last "Om" until my lungs scream out to breathe.

With the light out the black hole that was the window comes alive with stars, and wispy clouds float in the muted moonlight. Voices drift through the screen and I remember that odd lake effect that hollows out voices and projects the sound, like old echoes, in unseen waves of air. I shiver.

I pull the patchwork quilt from the bed, wrap it cape-like over my shoulders and settle in the small rocking chair by the window. From this angle I can see just the end of the Evers dock, where Fred stands with his hands in his pockets and his head thrown back. I almost expect him to howl at the moon as it emerges from the cloud edge and splashes the dock and the lake with light. The scene is contradictory. Things appear light that my brain knows are dark and the inverse, like a photographic negative. Carol joins Fred, triggering the motion detector and splashing artificial light across the scene. I watch them standing together, not quite touching, until the motion light goes out and the lake and the dock and Fred and Carol are swallowed by the darkness. I close my eyes.

* * *

Uncle Ed was gone for most of that day in late August. Gran had driven him to the VA for an appointment. Two of the shirt-tail cousins had gone into town for haircuts and taken cousin Fred and his mother with them. Helen had a headache and spent most of the day in bed. I took a screwdriver from the shoe box under the sink, placed it between the pages of my book. I filled an old fruit jar with water before taking my place in the boat with my false fishing pole, and waited. By noon the other cousins got tired of catching minnows on the shallow side of the dock and wandered down a few cottages to where several noisy neighbor children were swimming. I emptied the fruit jar into the lake. When I was sure there was no one watching I slipped to the back of the boat and worked loose the screw that let the gas drain out when the motor was stored for the winter. It was tighter than it had been when Cliff showed it to me the year before. The screwdriver slipped several times and scarred the paint on the old motor. But finally it turned and the gas spilled quickly, soaking the boat bottom before I could get the fruit jar under the hole. When the jar was nearly full I began turning the screw, leaving, I thought, just enough gas to get Uncle Ed out to his favorite fishing spot, but not enough to get back. And then I removed the inside screws that held the oar locks.

When the cousins returned I was sitting on the porch glider with a copy of Readers Digest and drinking a glass of lemonade. I couldn't possibly return the gasoline soaked copy of "Giants in the Earth" to the library, so I stashed it, with the screwdriver and the oar -lock screws in a metal candy box Gran gave me after Uncle Ed's swimming lesson, and hid it under the thorn bush out by the road. I'd bury it later. The snatched gasoline was safely back in the red can in the utility room, and the fruit jar, still smelling faintly of gas, sat innocently next to the others in the cabinet. I was almost relieved when Gran and Uncle Ed returned and the unnatural quiet of the afternoon was replaced by more normal door slamming and raised voices. Gran was busy getting something on for supper and Uncle Ed came out to the porch with his beer.

"Frederick Andrew Evers!" I heard Gran holler and then cousin Fred bolted through the door behind Uncle Ed. He winked as he ran past me and said, "No hot dogs tonight!"

"Frederick!" It was Gran. She stood at the door with a pair of long metal tongs and watched Freddie disappear around the corner of a neighboring cottage. "What is wrong with that boy? Why, he just threw a spider in the pot with the hot dogs I was boilin' up for supper. Now they're ruined. Why on earth would he do a thing like that?"

"Maybe he don't like spiders", Uncle Ed said. "Or hot dogs." I looked up to see him smiling then taking a long swig from his beer.

"Don't be silly," Gran said. "All kids - 'specially boys - love hot dogs. Dinner's ruined; what am I going to do now?"

Helen came out of Gran's bedroom, the tight forehead lines from her migraine relaxed, and her eyes able to focus, and suggested we all go to the Shoreline for dinner. All of the cousins and shirt tail cousins and Helen and Gran got cleaned up and walked together down the road to the Shoreline Resort. Uncle Ed didn't go. He planted himself in the glider with a six pack of beer and said, "Got my supper right here."

It wasn't until we got to the diner that Gran noticed I wasn't wearing shoes. The Shoreline had a "No Shirt, No Shoes, No Service" policy, but the waitress that used to serve Cliff and me our ice cream with sprinkles found a pair of rubber flip flops in the lost-and-found for me, and we all sat down to eat. It was the best day of that entire August. Everybody ordered what they wanted, some of the little cousins actually ordered hot dogs, and Cousin Fred tried to teach us all to hang spoons on our noses while we waited for our ice cream with sprinkles. I almost didn't mind being squeezed into a booth next to Gran, Helen even laughed out loud when Gran told a story about the time Helen and her brother Frank, Cousin Fred's father, put salt in the sugar bowl for April Fools and Grampa put three spoonfuls into his morning coffee. Then Gran said "So, little Fred here didn't get his penchant for pranks from no place strange, I guess." And everybody got quiet for a minute, Gran recalling the lingering illness that took her husband when she had three small children to raise, while others remembered the freak training accident that killed Uncle Frank, just last year. And then, just as the Shoreline's neon sign flickered on outside, Uncle Frank's widow said, "Yeah, that boy of mine sure is a chip of the old block all right." And everyone agreed.

It was dark when we all started back for the cottage. Gran said we shouldn't walk on the road in the dark so we headed for the lake shore. We walked across the beaches in front of the other cottages, saying Hi to neighbors we didn't even know. Well, Gran probably knew them. We were about half the way when suddenly somebody shot up a flare out on the water. We all stopped to watch it arc across the darkness. And just when it should have gone out and fallen, it burst into a million tiny sparks and rained down like shiny pebbles on the water. "Oh!" we all breathed together. Before the glowing image faded from the air another flare arched across the clouds and burst. And then another and another. We stopped and took places on the nearest dock and watched as the colors jumped into the sky and exploded into tiny shards of orange and yellow and red. All along the shoreline the cottages emptied and everyone oohed'd and ahhhh'd at the spectacle. The Fire Department did fireworks on the Fourth of July on the Big Lake, but nobody could remember anyone ever doing them on Little Crooked before. The display went on for almost forty minutes and then in a noisy grand finale multiple rockets flew up and burst, and many seemed to explode right there on the water, so many that the lake itself seemed to be on fire. And then the darkness closed over the last fading image, a tiny glow flickered on the water and was gone, and everything was still.

The smell of spent fireworks crawled across the water and seeped into our noses as we made our way back to Gran's cottage. We were tired and cold and climbed into our beds without bothering to put on our night clothes, without noticing that the sabotaged boat and Uncle Ed were both gone.

7

I wake to a dog barking and children yelling. Dream fragments, flashes of fireworks and the smell of cordite dissolve into daylight and I ache between my shoulder blades as I raise my head. I lean forward in the uncomfortable rocker and push myself to my feet. Once standing, I can see the dog outside, chasing a frisbee into the lake. I pull an ineffective lace curtain across the window, drag the quilt with me and lie down on the bed.

It's no use. The dog barking and the ache in my back won't let me sleep. I sit on the edge of the bed and contemplate my toes. A phone rings downstairs and I hear Carol's voice. I smell coffee and am surprised, when I look at my watch, that it is already past ten o'clock. I dress quickly and find Carol in the kitchen. She offers me coffee with her apology.

"I'm so sorry about the way I acted last night," she says. "I just wish Fred could see it the way I do. He and Bobby go back a long time, of course."

"Well," I say, adding some sugar and stirring the coffee. "It must have been hard, not knowing, for what, ten years? I can't even imagine how you must feel. Do they know how the accident happened?"

Carol looks at me sharply. "Fred didn't tell you about Charlene, did he?"

"No," I say, shaking my head slowly.

"The night Charlene disappeared - ran away, according to Bobby - she came to see me. She was scared. They were fighting again. They were always fighting, I don't know why they ever got married, except she got pregnant. Anyway this time it was real bad. Bobby was drinking again, and she said she was going to leave him for good."

I sip the coffee and watch Carol chew her lower lip and fight back the tears forming in her eyes.

"Fred and I were late for a Lamaze class. And it's not like this was the first time she'd threatened to leave him." She sniffs. "We never saw her again."

"I'm sorry."

"It wasn't an accident," she says.

We drink our coffee and watch the girls and the dog in the yard. Although they favor Carol the girls remind me of the Fred I knew as a child. The oldest has donned a ragged towel like a cape and is racing around the yard brandishing a stick. The younger one and the dog follow. The dog is a nondescript mongrel that defies the conventions of breed. How like cousin Fred to have a mutt, I think, as the dog snatches the cape and the chase changes direction.

"More coffee?" Carol asks as she pours herself half a cup.

"No, thanks," I say. "But do you have a phone book? I need to make a call."

"Of course," she says. She finds me the book and then takes her coffee outside where the girls soon surround her, begging her to play.

I look up the realtors in the business pages and match the information Helen has given me with the Chandler Agency. The paid ad is small and mentions both sales and rental management. I program the number in my cell phone first and then complete the call.

"Chandler Agency, how can I help you?" a cheery voice asks.

"Yvonne Potter, please."

"Who's calling, please?" The voice sounds less cheery.

"Molly Swain. We had an appointment yesterday but I was delayed. It's about my mother's cottage. My mother is Helen Swain."

"One moment please." I hear a muffled cough and some throat clearing and then a more conversational voice.

"Miss Swain, hello. Yvonne Potter here. So glad that you called. But I'm afraid I won't be able to meet with you today. Unavoidable, I'm sure you understand. Are you staying at Hill House? I can call you to reschedule."

"Oh no," I say. "I'm staying at the Evers. I'm sorry I don't know the number here but you can reach me on my cell phone."

"Fred and Carol Evers?" Her voice rises at least an octave.

"Yes."

"Well, I know their number. I'll call you, Miss Swain. Goodbye."

I don't realize she has hung up until I hear the dial tone. I flip the cell phone closed and clip it to my waistband, then join Carol and the girls on the dock.

"Just look at that!" Carol says, pointing to the pontoon wedged in the mud on the shore side of the dock. "I'll bet the lake has lowered at least a foot!"

"What happened?" I ask.

"Oh, it's the lock in Chandler. Some damn fool was in too much of a hurry to wait for the gates to go down. They busted up the mechanism that works the lock."

Does a foot really make that much difference?" I ask.

"Oh it's not just the lake level, it's that the lock is out of commission," Carol says, placing her hands on her hips and heaving a large sigh. "We're the gateway of the Inland waterway, you know. Lots of boats come through the locks, especially now that they're developing the North shore. It was one of the North Shore investors did the damage."

"Can it be fixed?"

Oh sure, but we have to wait on the State. And it's not just the DNR. The Army Corps of Engineers says we need to upgrade the lock but nobody's got the money to do it. They've been working on a temporary fix for a week now. Gotta do something soon, the water level just keeps going down and the summer season is just getting started.. Did you make your call?"

"Yes, she's going to call me back."

"Come on mom," the girls are calling from the other end of the dock. The dog is barking and jumping in and out of the boat.

"Well, the girls and I are going to take the rowboat out and do some fishing. I need to tell them about Kyle and Billy. They're not close, a couple of years is like forever when you're nine. But you can't keep secrets in small towns and I don't want them hearing about it from someone else. You're welcome to come along if you want. Fred says you used to spend half the summer fishing off the end of the dock when you were a kid."

"No," I say too quickly. And then seeing the question in her eyes I add, "I haven't fished in a really long time. Besides, you want to talk to the girls, and I'd be a distraction. I think I'll walk around the lake, see if I recognize the old cottage."

"Of course. How silly of me." She turns and yells to the girls. "Frieda you stow that gear tight his time, and take that dog back to the house, I am not going to take a dog fishing."

"Oh, mom." Charlene extends a pouty lower lip, looking so much like her father I have to laugh. "Oh, mom," the older girl chimes in.

"Oh, all right, but if he falls in you two can clean him up. Frieda, help Charlene with that life jacket, she's got the belt wrong again." She looks back and me and says, "That dog always falls in, jumps in if you ask me. We never catch any fish with him in the boat. Hey, why don't you join us down at the Shoreline tonight, around six? Fred won't be home till late, and we obviously aren't going to catch any dinner "

"It's a date," I say, and watch them push off from the dock, the dog still jumping and barking and the girls and Carol laughing at his antics. I stand on the dock until their laughter fades into the lapping waves against the dock. Lucky Fred, I think, looking back at the Evers' home and feeling a sharp twinge in my chest.

Why is it things work out for some folks and not for others? We were all little kids once, ate the same cereals and watched the same TV shows. So why is it life works out great for some, like cousin Fred, and doesn't work out at all for others, like me? We even have some of the same genes to work with. Of course, there is the gender thing. And, oh yeah, cousin Fred never killed anybody.

8

When I was little, Cliff and I walked around the lake on a path that passed by the backsides of several small cottages and then wandered a while along short stretches of uninhabited shoreline . Today I walk the shoulder of a paved two lane that takes me from Cousin Fred's to the abandoned cabins behind the Shoreline Diner. I try to remember how the cabins used to be. Their caved in roofs and gaping, doorless faces are ghostly and foreign. Only a jagged piece of peeling ginger bread trim hanging from the peak of one cabin and an overturned window box, its lattice sides curling into the weeds, give any clue to the charming little houses they used to be. I turn off the road near the corpselike cabins onto a well worn path toward the land bridge. Except for an abandoned stove rusting in the undergrowth, and a few bald tires alongside, the path through the wooded shoreline seems remarkably unchanged. I could almost be a child again, walking with cousin Fred or with Cliff around the lake.

I never cry. There's no advantage to it. Besides, when I was growing up Helen cried enough for both of us. Crying is something weak-knee'd, whiny people resort to. I never cry, so the wet streaming down my cheeks is a surprise. I swallow hard and feel the catch of that damned hook in my gullet.

"Shit!" I say, leaning my back against a tree and pulling my shirt collar up to wipe my face. "Shit!" The collar is ineffective and I rummage through my purse for a tissue. I had come here thinking I could find the tree and retrieve the box I had hidden so long ago. Now I just want to get away from the place. "Damn it , Helen" I think. But it isn't Helen's fault. I know that. It's me. When I was eleven I covered the box over, concealing it and my guilt, pushing those memories into the darkest corners of my mind. And here I am, twenty years later, ready to dig it up. Open up all the old wounds. I'm already remembering. Dreaming about Uncle Ed, and the row boat, and the fireworks. "Compulsion to confess," that's what psychologists call it. It's a plain old guilty conscience. "Shit!" I say, pushing myself away from the tree and walking quickly along the path.

A short distance ahead I see yellow streamers strung between the trees. The path itself is obstructed by a crisscross of yellow caution tape. I am about to turn around when I hear Fred's voice.

"Hey, Molly. That you Molly?"

I sniff and swallow hard to clear my eyes to present a good face, then turn to see Fred lumbering down the path toward me.

"You okay?" he asks, narrowing his eyes and cocking his head to one side.

"Allergies," I apologize, holding up the tissue as evidence and sniffing again. "What's all this?"

"C-S-I," he says urging me to follow him down the path toward the tapes. "You know, Crime Scene Investigation. Geeze Molly, don't writers watch television?"

"Not me anyway," I say, following him. Now I can see that there are several people on the other side of the tape. Some have rakes and others are simply walking, staring at the ground in front of them. Two young officers seem to be arguing over a piece of equipment that looks like a small electric broom.

"Hey!" Fred hollers at them. "Get that thing going or get it out of here."

"What are they doing?" I ask, wiping my eyes and putting the tissue in my pants pocket.

"Looking for evidence," Fred says. "They aren't going to find any, but we have to look. Ever since we got that damn metal detector those two have been itchin' to use it."

Metal detector? I choke back a scream. A metal detector. They're going to find the box.

"Damn waste of resources," Fred says.

"Why?" I squeak.

"You writin' this up for a magazine?" he asks suddenly.

"No. No, I'm just curious."

"Because there's no way that car got through these trees to the lake, that's why. In December and January the ice is pretty thick. Lots of folks drive their snowmobiles and small trucks out onto the lake to set up their ice fishing shanties. Kids do it for thrills, doing donuts on the ice is pretty exciting when you're sixteen. Mustang isn't a very big car. My guess is, it came across the lake and hit a spot of shallow ice and went through. Joe Purdy over to the DNR says it could have gone through fifty or sixty yards out and drifted here slowly over the last ten years. Not all that unusual. Had the hull of an old boat wash up on the beach a couple of houses down from us last year. Figure it was one went down some fifteen years back during a storm. Broke away from it's moorings and just disappeared, till last year. So, anyway, there isn't going to be any evidence here, but we gotta go by the book, gotta cover all the bases."

"Yeah," I say, watching the two men with the metal detector sweep through the trees.

"It's okay, Molly." Fred says softly. "I know."

"You know?" I look up at Fred's face. How could he know?

"It's Cliff, isn't it? You're walking around the lake like you and Cliff did when we were kids. I know Molly. Sometimes I go over and stand on the dock at Gran's old place, where I remember my dad skipping stones with me before the accident. I just stand there like a goof, till somebody notices me or it gets to dark to see. It's okay. Really. Listen, the trail is closed off for the investigation, but I'll walk you through. Privilege of rank." He lifts the caution tape and we walk under it.

"Thanks," I tell Fred. "Thanks."

I come out of the trees on the other end of the land bridge and the path opens into the gravel road that leads to Crooked Lake Road where I found the boy. A faint path angles off to the right and I see Little Crooked through the trees and several small cottages hugging the shore. I look back toward the crime scene. Well then, I'm to be found out. It's a relief really. No more nightmares. No more jumping at shadows. No more fishhooks yanking out my innards. Just a matter of time now. They'll find the box, put two and two together, and it will be over. I follow the path until it widens out and merges with the paved road behind the cottages of Little Crooked. I walk on the dusty shoulder and wonder what Helen will think when she finds out, and then I see it.

I recognize the cottage immediately. Even with the overgrown bushes and several layers of peeling paint, the bones of my Grandmother Evers' storybook cottage are unmistakable. The tall peaked entry with its irregular sloped roof is partially obscured by two tall pine trees. They appear to be volunteers. The small roadside yard, where Gran used to plant rosebushes and rhododendrons, is thick with pines. A stone path beneath a layer of pine needles leads both to the door and around the cottage to the lake front. Although it looks deserted, I decide to go around to the front and look through the windows before venturing inside.

Several broken beach chairs lean against the faded siding of the cottage and three of the four panes in the kitchen window are broken. I step over some dented minnow buckets and a cache of rusted soup cans to get to the beach. The water lines on the dock piers indicate a water loss of only a few inches and although the rowboat moored to this dock is touching the sandy bottom, it is merely disturbing the sand, sending tiny clouds of debris to the surface as it rocks, not yet digging itself in like Fred's pontoon on the big lake. Out across the water the sun sparkles and the tiny wavelets curl back like a zillion taunting fingers, beckoning me. I shiver, remembering Uncle Ed and the 'swimming lesson.' I can swim now, and do, thanks to a sympathetic middle school phys ed teacher, who stayed late and patiently worked to calm my fear of the water and save me from the ridicule of my classmates. I can swim now, but only in swimming pools, never in lakes.

"Hey!" A man's voice behind me barks. "What are you doing?"

I turn to see a man in bib overalls and a baseball cap, standing on the path beside the cottage. He is shirtless and has a tool belt slung across one shoulder. Before I can think what to say he steps forward and says, "Miss Swain?"

Now I know the voice, though without the uniform I would never have recognized Officer Campion.

"What are you doing here?" he asks again.

None of your damned business, I think. But he is a policeman so I say "Betsy Evers was my grandmother. This is my mother's property."

"Really?" He takes off the ball cap, scratches behind one ear, then replaces the cap, pulling the bill down hard.

"Yes, really. What are you doing here?"

"I work part time for Chandler Realty. Fix broken windows, plumbing, things like that. Repaired the roof here last year. I thought the realty owned it. Sorry."

"They manage the rentals," I tell him. "I just wanted to see the old place. Do you have keys? I'd like to take a look inside."

"Yeah," he says, "I got the glass in my truck to fix the windows, okay with you if I get to it? I have to pick up my boy pretty soon."

"Oh, by all means," I say, and follow him around to where his truck is parked half in the yard, arms of the wild pine trees poking in the passenger window and reaching into the cluttered truck bed. "The better it looks the more we can get for it."

He retrieves a package from the front seat and turns to face me. "You're selling it?"

"Well, my mother is. That's why I'm here. To do the paperwork."

"Damn shame." he says, looking like I just shot his pet skunk.

"What's that?"

"Selling it. This place is one of the few original cottages that's still standing. That hasn't been renovated to death anyway. Progress!" he huffs and pulls a small toolbox out of the truck bed. "C'mon, don't have all day."

I follow him to the roadside door. He leans the package carefully against the wall and uses both hands to work the lock. Then he pushes open the door and ushers me through. Even before my eyes adjust to the dimmer light he is unwrapping the glass and setting to work on the window. Gran's cottage hasn't changed much. The furniture is different and Gran's old gas range has been replaced with a tiny apartment size electric one, but the knotty pine paneling is the same and the wide plank hardwood floor is too. The whole place is covered in a blanket of dust, as if the house has been sleeping a long time.

Three mismatched doors on the wall to my left mark the two small bedrooms and the tiny bathroom we all shared twenty years ago. There are dark rectangles on the paneling where pictures once hung. In fact, there is a picture still hanging on the far wall. The frame, I see, is screwed to the wall. I use the tissue from my pocket to wipe away the dust and there we are. Betsy Evers' clan. Gran is sitting in a director's chair with a fat toddler in her arms. Fred, I suppose. Behind her a smiling couple I assume to be cousin Fred's father, Frank , and his mother, Aunt Harriet, Next to Frank stands a tall good looking boy in a military uniform and next to him, Helen. Helen looks timid and vulnerable and incredibly young. They all look young, even Gran. And the tiny bundle of blankets that Helen holds so tightly, I realize, is me. I touch the dusty glass that covers Helen and swallow hard. I don't look like any of them, Helen least of all. Where she is petite and strikingly blond, I am tall and my hair is best described as dishwater brown. Even my green eyes defy the family genes. For a moment I wonder if the uniformed boy is my father, then remember he abandoned her before I was born. I look at the fresh face of the soldier and his strong hand on the back of Gran's chair. It's Uncle Ed, of course it is. It's a family picture. Gran and her children and grandchildren. Helen and her brothers. I back away, bumping a chair and bruising my shin, resisting the familiar pull that's dragging me toward my nightmare.

"Everything okay?" Campion asks from the kitchen where he has removed the window frame.

"Fine!" I manage to say, turning so he can't see my face and moving toward the open door. Outside I inhale deeply and let the pine scented air fill my lungs. The tears aren't just leaking out now, they are running down my face in heavy streams. I hear the cottage door open as I stumble down the roadway, but I don't look back and he doesn't follow.

I go the wrong direction and don't realize it until I see the cluster of buildings that make up the village of Cascade. By now the crying has stopped and I am working to calm the cramped thumping in my chest. It's nearly noon and I realize I haven't eaten. I buy a bottle of water and a couple of chocolate cupcakes at the convenience store on the main corner and sit on a bench in the waterfront park behind the store. My cell phone chirps out "turkey in the straw" and I struggle to unclip it from my belt. It's Helen. I let the phone lay in my palm and study the unanswered LED display until the song stops and Helen disappears. I stare out at the blue-green stretch of lake, lick cupcake filling from my fingers, and think.

Helen didn't cry when we buried Uncle Ed. There was a lot of crying and nose blowing, though. Gran shed buckets, and Aunt Harriet went around dabbing her eyes and sniffling. And even cousin Fred got choked up when Gran gave him Ed's fishing rod and called him the 'man in the family' now. But not Helen. Maybe she was just 'all cried out.' After all, she'd lost her dear brother Frank the year before, and then the next year she lost Cliff, the love of her life, and then Ed, her only other sibling.

I sort of remember Uncle Ed's funeral. The family all huddled under a big white tent. Some had chairs, like Helen and Gran. I stood behind Helen's chair. During the night a spider had spun a web between the brass rail on the coffin table and the ground. It was a splendid web. The sun caught tiny beads of morning dew on the thin strings of spider silk and sparkled them as it moved slowly across the sky. A bunch of other people gathered near the tent, the sheriff's deputy and some of the summer people. "Ed's friends," Helen said. When I was eleven I didn't think people like Uncle Ed had any friends. But the good looking boy in the photograph in Gran's cottage was different. That 'Ed' probably had lots of friends. And they came to Uncle Ed's funeral and sniffed and looked sad, and I remember one of the men actually came up and took Helen's hand. He said, "You probably don't remember me, I'm Skip, Skip Foster. I went to high school with Ed." Funny I should remember his name after all these years. I had to wear a dress, I remember that. And the shoes I was supposed to wear, patent leather Mary Janes that Gran picked up at Good Will, were too small so I got to wear my comfy brown sandals. Gran glared at me something fierce during the service, like I grew bigger feet just to spite her.

I remember the service was incredibly long. The spider caught three flies and a grasshopper before they lowered Ed into the ground and destroyed all of her hard work. I must have choked or something, because someone hugged me and somebody else said, "oh, poor child. Poor, poor child." Helen turned then and looked at me strangely and I guessed it would be better not to tell anyone that I was weeping for the spider who just lost her home. Some men from the local VFW gave Gran the American flag they folded into a tight triangle, while another one played taps on a trumpet. I nearly jumped into the hole with Uncle Ed's casket when some of the uniformed men raised their rifles and shot in the air. I caught cousin Fred's eye as we walked back to the cars. He took a spoon out of his pocket, breathed on it and hung it from his nose. I guess I must have smiled. Helen frowned and hurried me into the car. I saw Aunt Harriet take the spoon and cuff Freddie along side his head, as our car pulled away. Good old cousin Fred.

The cell phone beeps. I look down at the blinking LOW BATT signal, then back out at the blue green expanse of lake and wonder what Helen wanted.

9

Back at Fred's, Carol and the girls are still out on the boat. I plug my fading cell phone into the charger on my nightstand, find a couple of cookies in a crock in the kitchen and pour myself a glass of milk. I wander, cookie and milk in hand, around the main floor of the house admiring pictures of the Evers' children from infant to a fairly recent photo of Fred and the girls in Little League uniforms. I'm not snooping. Fred's home feels like a warm and comforting quilt and I'm just wrapping myself in it. Carol's taste in art runs to watercolor still life, and several of them are displayed in a small library/office off the living room. The one nearest the door is a very small painting of a yellow bowl filled with red cherries on a white crocheted doily. It's absolutely exquisite. I lean in to look at the intricate laces of the doily and see the signature. C. Evers. I look quickly around the room at the other still life. C. Evers, C. Evers, C. Evers. They are all Carol's. And they are good enough to be in a gallery somewhere. I walk back to the kitchen, wishing I too had a hidden talent. It is almost two o'clock when I rinse out the glass and set it, bottom up, on the drain board and look out with window at the lake.

Across the water, I imagine I can see Fred's crime scene officers and wonder if the metal detectors have uncovered my little box of horrors yet. Oddly, I don't feel any tug of guilt or remorse. I can even think about it clearly now. I killed Uncle Ed. No officer, it wasn't an accident. I deliberately sabotaged the boat, hoping to strand Uncle Ed on the lake. Did I mean to kill him? A tiny little tug in my chest. I'm not sure. I was angry enough. I could plead self defense, of course. Uncle Ed did try to drown me. Or was it the dog Uncle Ed "put out of its misery" that made me do it?

Whether it is weariness or relief, I'm not sure, but I am suddenly very tired. I stumble up the stairs and stop in the bathroom to wash up. I am surprised at how ordinary my face in the picture frame mirror appears. Somehow I had expected that once the mask of my criminal childhood was revealed, it would show in my face. Some evil twitch or telling scar where at last the hook of my guilt would poke through. It is disconcerting to realize how normal I look. If I could look so innocent, then anyone could be a murderer. Anyone.

I dream almost as soon I close my eyes. I am standing in Gran's cottage staring at the faded photo of Betsy Evers and her children and grandchildren securely attached to the living room wall. While I watch, the picture grows larger and larger, until the people in it are life size. And then it isn't Gran's cottage anymore, but a long hallway, like a gallery and the dark rectangles on the paneled walls become similar pictures of other people I know. Fred and Carol, Officer Campion, Helen and Cliff, the paramedics from yesterday. And then, one by one, they are lifting masks up to their faces and stepping out of their frames. The hallway becomes crowded with people and masks. They begin to dance and I am swept clumsily into a sea of figures moving across the floor. There is no music but the figures seem locked in a universal rhythm, all moving to the same cadence, all listening to the same song. I have a mask in my hand too, and as I lift it to cover my face I begin to move in harmony with the other figures. We float, a sea of colors and shapes. I can see only masks now, the people behind them have faded away.

The littlest girl, Charlene, wakes me. "Aunt Molly, Aunt Molly, my mom says to wake up," she says, poking my arm with her finger. The parade of masks recedes and the bright face of Charlene Evers floats inches from my eyes. "Aunt Molly, wake up."

"Up," I say thickly. "I'm up."

"She's awake!" Charlene yells, then she runs from the room. "She's awake!" I hear her yelling as she runs down the stairs. I open my eyes and focus on the room. Am I? I wonder.

I feel like I've slept for days but according to my watch it's only been about an hour. The sun is still shining and I've hardly disturbed the quilt on the bed. Downstairs the girls are making a lot of noise and I hear Carol admonishing Charlene for waking me.

"I'm sorry" she says as I come down the stairs. "The girls are anxious to get to the Shoreline. I told them we'd go when you woke up. I did not tell them to wake you."

"That's okay," I tell her, checking to make sure I have cash in my wallet. I left my purse and the half charged cell phone on the nightstand. I'm not expecting any calls, and I don't want Helen to spoil this evening for me. "I didn't mean to fall asleep, anyway, and I'm absolutely starving."

We walk the same path I'd taken earlier, along the paved road toward the Shoreline. Carol and I walk slowly, the girls racing ahead then dropping back and then racing ahead again. Fred called while I was sleeping and told Carol he'd meet us at the diner. Carol is busy alternately telling Frieda not to get too far ahead and Charlene not to pick up things on the roadside. Free from the responsibility of conversation I am enjoying the warm afternoon sun, the variety of flowering weeds along the roadside and a euphoric feeling of well being. The colors of the flowers blooming in the yards we pass seem brighter to me now, the textures more distinct. It is a sensation like a slow motion reel unwinding in my head, and I can almost distinguish each individual frame. Maybe this is that clarity that I read about while waiting for my last dentists appointment. In the article, terminal patients described a heightened sensitivity, and people who fasted frequently reported a similar phenomena. It was an odd magazine for a dentist office, I thought at at time. Now it just seems like one of those cosmic coincidences that you remember after the fact.

The girls reach the doors of the restaurant and look back at us. "Go ahead," Carol calls to them, and they disappear inside. They stake out the big circular booth in the back and the waitress fills their water glasses. Carol hesitates at a table nearer the door. I see the boy first, his head bandaged and the orange traces of mercurochrome on the scratches on his arms. His hair is neatly combed and his eyes never leave his folded hands on the table.

"Hi Will," Carol says and I notice the uniform as Officer Campion rises to acknowledge us. "You know Fred's cousin, Molly."

"Ma'am," he says nodding in my direction. The boy looks up briefly, and then down again at his hands.

"How are you doing, Billy?" Carol leans down and tries to see Billy's eyes. He does not respond. She looks up at Officer Campion. "You know Will, it might be nice for Billy to come out and stay with us for a few days. You'd like that, wouldn't you Billy? The girls could double up and you could bunk in Charlene's room. Molly's in the guest room, or you could bunk there."

Billy sits rigidly silent, but suddenly Yvonne blurts. "Molly? Are you Helen's daughter?"

"Why, yes," I say.

"Oh, I'm sorry," Will Campion says. "Molly this Yvonne. Yvonne, Molly."

"Yes Yvonne," I say. "We talked earlier, remember?I look forward to meeting with you."

"Yes, yes." Yvonne taps the side of her water glass with long red fingernails. Next to her, Billy begins to squirm in his seat. She stops tapping and holds the glass firmly. "I'll be available tomorrow morning if you can come by the office. Say tenish? Would that work for you?"

"Fine," I tell her. "That would be fine."

"Will," Carol says suddenly, nodding at Billy's bowed head and then looking over at the booth where her girls are laughing and shooting straw papers at each other. "Why don't you join us?

"We were just leaving," Yvonne rushes to say. She turns to pull her jacket off the chair back and picks up her purse.

"I'm on duty tonight," Will Campion explains. "But thanks. And Carol, if it wouldn't be too much trouble, I'll take you up on your offer. I don't want him to be alone, but we're short staffed and I have to go work. Yvonne can take him home and pack up some of his things and drop him off later tonight, if that's okay."

"We'd love to have him." Carol says, smiling. "See you later, then, Billy."

As we walk between the tables toward our booth, I watch Officer Campion and Yvonne Potter's reflections in the mirrored panels above the booths. The boy stands rigidly next to his father while Officer Campion pays the check and talks in low tones with Yvonne. She lays her purse on the counter and roughly punches her hands through the sleeves of her jacket. He attempts to help her but she pulls away.

I remember my jacket, turn toward them and call out. "Officer Campion?"

They both stop and look at me across the diner.

"My jacket." I say. "Do you know what they did with my jacket?"

For a moment he looks blank, then he looks at Billy and nods his head. "I'll check," he says.

I turn back toward Carol and the boys, but not before I see a scowl cross Yvonne's face. It changes quickly to a imitation smile and then a short stuttered laugh as I watch her reflection link arms with Officer Campion as he pushes his wallet into a back pocket and they leave the restaurant with Billy in tow. Poor Billy, I think. Poor Officer Campion.

"What'll you have?" The waitress asks as I slide into the booth beside Frieda.

The girls order burgers and Carol orders pork chops. I study the menu while the girls beg their mother for quarters for the ancient Pac Man game near the restrooms. I order the soup and sandwich combo with a strawberry soda.

"You look kinda familiar," the waitress says. "Have you been in before?"

"A long time ago," I tell her. "Twenty years or more."

"Well," the woman says, and takes our orders to the grill.

The girls are flipping scrunched up straw papers at each other across the table when their father arrives. "Hey Flo!" he says cheerfully to the waitress as he passes the cash register. "Put on a steak special for me, will ya?

The waitress nods and Fred stops at several tables to shake hands or say hello. He slides into the booth next to Carol. "Mind if I join you two beautiful ladies. Who are these two hooligans with you?"

"Oh dad," the girls moan in unison. He gives each girl two quarters and they wiggle out of the booth and race off to the Pac-Man game. He and Carol rearrange themselves on the bench and the waitress brings him a cup and pours coffee into it.

"I remember you now," she says nodding at me. She stands next to Fred with the coffee pot in her hand. "You're Betsy Evers granddaughter, by God. You and your dad used to come in for ice cream, The professor, right?"

"Right," I say looking more closely at the waitress. She's a tall woman in her middle fifties, I guess. No make up, sensible shoes. I try to imagine her twenty years younger and come up blank.

"Well, if that don't beat all. You know I used to date your Uncle Ed. Course that was a long time ago. I'll bet you don't remember, but the night of the accident your whole family, nearly twenty of you came in here for dinner. I found you a pair of beach shoes in the lost and found cause you forgot your shoes."

"You remember that?"

"Oh hell yes, I remember that night like it was yesterday. That night changed my whole life." A bell sounded in the kitchen and Flo went to fetch an order.

"I can't believe she remembers me." I tell Fred. The girls have used up their quarters and come back to the booth. I move over to make room for Frieda on the bench, Charlene crawls under the table and comes up on my other side. "Who remembers you?" Charlene asks.

"Aunt Molly and I used to come here when we were kids." Fred tells them. They both sit up straight like an electric shock has run through them. I think that Fred has told them many stories about his youth, because they both lean forward and Frieda says, "You knew my dad when he was a little boy?" "What was he like?" Charlene. asks.

"Oh no, my secrets out at last. Go ahead Molly, tell them." He hangs his head in mock shame and Carol just smiles.

"Well," I begin. "I remember that your dad used to make me laugh all the time. Did you know that he can balance a spoon on his nose?"

The girls grab the spoons off the table and quickly hang them from own noses.

"An inherited skill," Fred assures me, smiling.

"And once," I lower my voice conspiratorially, "he threw a spider in with the hot dogs our Gramma Evers was cooking for our dinner. She threw the whole pot out and we came here to the Shoreline for dinner."

"Euuuuuu," they chorus.

All through our dinner I watch cousin Fred interacting with his children. He distracts Carol and steals green beans off her plate. The girls dissolve in giggles. He drops his napkin and asks Frieda to please get it. While she is retrieving the napkin Fred takes several french fries from her plate. When Frieda sees our faces, trying hard not to smile, she glances over the table but can't figure out what's changed, until Charlene blurts out "Did you eat all your French fries, Freddie?" We eat ice cream for dessert, and Flo searches the kitchen for sprinkles, although she tells us, "We only put sprinkles on the cupcakes now, but for you . . ."

Watching Fred and his family has made me even more aware of my own disconnect. My relationships with men have all been disastrous. The thought of children scares the hell out me. But Fred's family. Well, if things were different, it would give me hope that someday I'd find someone too. I try, but I can't enjoy the memories that ice cream with sprinkles ought to evoke. I look at Cousin Fred over my spoonful of ice cream. Surely if they'd found my box he would have told me by now. Maybe it's the wrong kind of metal I reason. Or maybe somebody already found it. A chill races down my back as I put the ice cream in my mouth and swallow, hard.

10

I'm early and I see that it annoys Yvonne Potter. Last night, when Campion brought his son to Carol's, he said Yvonne had developed a bad headache and couldn't drive. She looks okay today. While she talks on the phone with a client, I wander around the small office looking at pictures of houses and maps tacked to the walls. Will Campion is probably right about Gran's place being the last of the original cottages. Several of the displayed pictures are the before-and-after kind that people do when they remodel. Maybe it's just because they are more familiar to me, but I think that most of them look better in the before pictures.

Apparently Chandler Real Estate shares its office with North Shore Development. Several large site maps on rickety easels show the proposed development on the little lake. One of the maps shows the existing properties and several of them have large red x's slashed across them. I run my finger around the blue line that defines the lake shore, and attempt to find Gramma Evers cottage among the red marks.

"Well, Miss Swain. Molly." Yvonne's professional voice sweeps across the room before the phone's receiver clunks into it's cradle. "Thank you for coming in this morning. It must be terribly hard for you."

"Excuse me?" I say, turning away from the maps.

"Please, sit down," she says, indicating one of the soft leather chairs across from her desk. "Yes, William told me about the accident. It must have been quite a shock."

"William?" I ask as I sit down in one of them and drop my purse in the other.

"Officer Campion," she says, smiling and adjusting the silver bracelet on her wrist. "We've been dating for some time now, we're practically engaged." She smiles again. "He mentioned that you were the one who called nine-one-one. I get chills just thinking about that poor boy."

"Billy does seem to be quite upset."

"Not Billy. I mean the other boy. They say he's in a coma. It's just heartbreaking. Heartbreaking. Poor Mr. Matthews. You know his wife left him? Just up and walked out one day, left him with that little baby. And now to have this horrible accident. It's just too sad." Yvonne pulls a tissue, from the chimney of a needle worked box shaped like a house on the corner of her desk, and sniffles delicately into it. "Well, we have work to do don't we. Have you been to the county records office yet?"

"Excuse me?"

"Well Miss Swain, we can't do anything until the deed is cleared. I thought you knew. It's a good offer, considering the condition of the property. The money is already in an escrow account, including the closing costs. So once the deed is cleared, and the seller - that's your mother - signs the paperwork I can issue a check immediately. I'm sure you want to get back to your life as soon as possible."

"I'm sorry, Yvonne. Helen didn't tell me anything. I don't even know what the offer is. And what's the problem with the deed?"

"Oh my, I thought this was all clear." Yvonne searches though a file drawer and pulls out a yellow file folder. While she spreads it open on the desk she smiles up at me. "The buyer's offer is twenty-eight thousand, plus closing costs, and takes the property 'as is.' That means no inspections or anything."

She looks down and runs a long red fingernail down the document in front of her. "Yes, here it is. The deed isn't properly titled. That's the problem. You will need to get the deed re-titled before we can complete the sale."

"What's wrong with the title?" I ask.

"Well, I'm not entirely sure, Molly. But I think that one of the titled owners is deceased. I'd guess that you have to get a copy of the death certificate and file it with the county."

"Helen never took Gramma Evers off the title?" How like Helen. If this had been part of the Swain Trust it would have been done years ago. I would have done it.

"You'll have to ask the county clerk. Once you have clear title we can go forward with the sale. It's a really good offer, Molly, considering the condition of the property, I mean."

"About that," I say. "I went by the cottage yesterday and it's pretty run down. It doesn't look like it's been rented in a while either."

Yvonne folds her hands in her lap and leans back in her chair.

"Well, rental properties do take a beating, you know. And rentals have been down the last couple of years. The economy, I suppose. That's why this offer is so timely. Summer cottages are just not the vacation-of-choice anymore."

"So, why would anyone want to buy it?"

"Oh it's not the cottage he wants, Molly. It's the land."

My cell phone begins playing "turkey in the straw" and I apologize as I rummage in my purse to find it. It's Helen. I flip open the phone and smile apologetically at Yvonne as I say "Hello" into the receiver.

"Where are you?" Helen's voice trills so loudly that even Yvonne winces from it.

"Actually, I'm in the realty office in Chandler. Where you sent me, remember?"

"Why didn't you answer your phone? I called three times yesterday."

"Well, I ran into a little trouble yesterday, and the cell reception up here is pretty iffy, Helen. If I'm not right in town, it doesn't work at all."

"Trouble?" Helen squeaks. "What happened? Did you crash your car?"

Of course Helen would expect the "trouble" was my fault. Not 'are you all right?' but 'did you crash the car'. "No, there was an accident but I wasn't involved. It delayed things, that's all. Oh," I say to change the subject, "I ran into cousin Fred."

"Harriet's boy?" Helen sounds wistful.

"Yeah, I'm staying at his place, with his family."

She doesn't take the bite. Her natural curiosity about Fred's family and how she could use such information to needle me about my inadequacies goes unspoken. All she says is, "Oh, well say hello for me."

"Sure, listen Helen, do you have a title or a deed for the cottage?"

"Deed? Her voice is substantially lower now and Yvonne leans forward unconsciously in her chair.

I turn slightly and cradle the phone with my shoulder. Yvonne realizes she is intruding and picks up a file to cover her gaff. She sits back in her chair as I ask Helen, "What about a tax statement, or an assessment?"

"I don't save that stuff Molly. I just pay the bill when it comes, like always."

"Okay. I guess I'll have to go to the county clerk's office and see if they can help me. Helen?"

"What?"

"What did you want?"

"What?"

"When you called me. You said you called three times yesterday. What did you want?"

"Oh," she says softly. "Nothing. It can wait. Bye."

Dial tone buzzes in my ear. "Okay, Bye" I tell it.

"Sorry about that," I tell Yvonne as I close the phone. "where were we?"

Yvonne lays the folder she's been holding, open, on the desk and clears her throat, but before she can speak "turkey in the straw" fills the room again.

"Excuse me," I say. "This never happens." The number calling isn't one I know, but it's local, so I answer questioningly. "Hello?"

"Miss Swain?" a pleasant male voice inquires.

"Yes." I say. "Who is this?"

"Will Campion, Miss Swain. Billy's dad. I'm calling about your jacket."

"Oh yes, Mr. Campion. I'm surprised to hear from you." I hear Yvonne's nails rapping the desktop.

"You gave me your card, remember?"

"Oh, yes. Yes, I remember now."

"You'll have to go to the hospital administration office and sign for your jacket. Do you know where Chandler Memorial is?"

"I can find it, thank you. I'll be there this afternoon."

"And Miss Swain . . . Molly. . ."

"Yes?"

"Thanks."

"I'm sorry?"

"I've been wanting to thank you. For stopping to help my son. And then, you know, sticking around and helping with

Kyle. Some folks would have just kept on driving. Although Fred tells me you're not like most folks. He says they broke the mold after they made you, and he means it in a nice way. And I think so too Molly. Miss Swain. So, anyway, um. I wanted to tell you, that's all. Thank you."

The rush of Officer Campion's words pushes the polite response mechanism I have perfected to keep people at a distance back down my throat. I move my mouth but nothing comes out.

"Are you there? Molly?"

"Yes!" I reply. He thinks you're "not like most folks," "in a nice way." For god sake Molly say something! "You're welcome . . . Will. Officer Campion. And . . . thank you."

I flip the cell phone closed and hold it a moment, thinking about the odd thing that just happened, before I stuff it back into my purse. Then I look up to catch Yvonne staring at me. She looks away almost instantly, but she closes the file folder in her hand and raps the lower edge of it repeatedly into the desk.

"Thank you, Yvonne." I say, squirming to get out of the plump leather chair. "I have some other errands to do, I'll call you as soon as I make the changes to the deed. Okay?"

"Fine," Yvonne says slapping the folder on top of a stack of folders on the desk.

11

On the sidewalk outside the Realty, I stand for a moment in the warm sunshine. Officer Campion's voice resonates through my head, pushing Helen's cryptic "It can wait." into the shadows. Rustic storefronts and colorful awnings line the street, signs of progress I suppose. Cars slow for a woman pushing a double stroller across the street. She turns and waves as they pass by. A few storefronts away a door opens and the smell of fresh baked bread and cinnamon rolls rushes out. A man steps out carrying paper coffee cups in a holder. He holds the door for the woman behind him, who balances a bakery box while she shoulders a large tote bag. They pass me and I inhale the hypnotic fumes. I could use a cup of coffee. I'm almost at the door of the bakery when I see the "HOSPITAL" sign at the end of the block, it's arrow pointing slightly uphill. I recall the low sprawling hospital, converted from an elementary school before my time, just a few blocks off Main Street. Every summer we made at least one trip to the emergency room. A cousin who stepped on a nail. A sprained ankle. Even waiting once for Helen, when a migraine required more than the usual treatment. Through the bakery window I can see there's a long line. I could pick up my jacket and come back for a relaxing cup of coffee when there's less of a crowd.

The sprawling infirmary is gone, or at least camouflaged. Covered with scaffolds and canvas and construction fence, Chandler Memorial is a three story work in progress. Stacks of wood and brick cover the area between the sidewalk and the building. Workmen installing a window dangle on a scaffold three stories up. Traffic cones mark a temporary parking area and funnel visitors through the emergency entrance. I pass an electronic sensor in the wall and the wide doors swing in, pulling me into the cool, antiseptic-scented waiting room. The plain wood benches where I waited for Helen and Gran to identify Uncle Ed's remains, have been replaced with tubular steel and red upholstery. I hurry along the wide hallway. The curtained cubicles are much as I remember them. A gruff old doctor once pulled a barbed fishing hook from my thumb and jammed a tetanus syringe into my butt cheek in one of them. I walk faster, sensing the elevators, just ahead. Administration is on the third floor.

I step off the elevator as two uniformed policemen leave an office. Too late to turn around, the elevator is already gone. One officer carries a paper grocery bag with a yellow sticker that says "EVIDENCE" across the top. It's my box, I'm sure of it. They hold the heavy glass door for me and I actually shiver as I walk past them. My mouth is dry and I swallow hard trying to dislodge the guilty knot in my throat. Before the woman sitting at the reception desk can greet me, cousin Fred emerges from one of the offices behind her.

"Molly!" he says and then looks back into the office. "Hey Howard, come on out and meet my cousin Molly."

"So glad to meet you, Molly," Howard says vigorously shaking my hand. "Fred's been telling us all about you. Actually, it turns out we kind of know each other."

"We do?" I ask, swallowing hard. Howard is a short, stocky man with dark curly hair. He has a sort of friendly spaniel quality about him, but he doesn't look at all familiar.

"Yep. Well, I don't know that we ever actually met, you understand. My folks had a summer cottage on Little Crooked, just a few down from your Grandmother's. Santini's?"

I shake my head.

"Well, I don't blame you for not remembering, there were nine of us kids. Six boys and three girls. Heck I wouldn't have remembered myself, except Fred here was asking me about the summer that fella doin' the fireworks drowned. You were that little skinny gal that read books while you were fishin', right. Say, that fella, Ed something, he was a relative of yours, wasn't he?

"My mother's brother," I say looking at Fred in time to catch him motioning to Harold. He stops with his hand halfway across his neck, lets it fall to his chest and clears his throat.

"Molly," Fred stammers. "What, uh, what are you doing here?"

"My jacket," I tell him. "Officer Campion said that I could pick it up here. When I found that boy in the road he was cold and shivering. I covered him with my jacket. The paramedics took it when they brought him in."

"Miss Swain?" the receptionist asks. We all turn as she pulls a plastic bag from her desk drawer. "I think this is what you want. Will said you'd be by. He wanted to take it to be cleaned first, but I told him I could only release it to the proper owner. Hospital policy, you know. I just need you to sign a release."

While I sign for the jacket, Fred talks quietly to Harold in the doorway of Harold's office. When I'm done, Harold waves quietly and slips back into his office. Fred takes my elbow and guides me toward the elevators.

"So, Molly. What do you think of our 'cube?' he asks.

"Cube?"

The hospital. It's like one of those puzzle cubes, you know. You twist it to mess up the colors and then try to put them back together. Harold likes it. Since they moved his office up here, he says he can see practically everything going on in town."

"Rubic's Cube?"

"Yeah, like that. The whole damn place is color coded. Admin is blue, cardio pulmonary is green, emergency is red, maternity is lavender. It's supposed to be efficient. My office is the only white space in the whole building. I took the designer down there to discuss the decor and made sure he knew a morgue needed to be white. Should'a seen his face while I described an autopsy."

"Fred?" I say as he leans to push the elevator button.

"Yeah?"

"Why were you asking Harold about the summer Uncle Ed died?"

The elevator bell rings and the doors open. Fred moves toward them. I stand firmly with my arms across the plastic bundle of my jacket. "Well?" I say.

"I guess you have a right to know," Fred says. He stops the elevator door from closing with one hand and motions for me to enter with the other. "I was about to go to lunch. Come with me and I'll tell you what I know."

I follow Fred to the hospital cafeteria. It's lunchtime and the room is a sea of pastel uniforms. We pick up trays and join the line of aides and nurses scooting their trays across the metal rails toward the cashier. I pick up a some crackers and decide on the homemade bean soup. The woman behind the counter ladles it carefully into a brown crockery bowl and smiles as she hands it to me. There are pies on glass shelves as I scoot my tray down the line, every kind of pie I can imagine. I pick a large slice of banana cream, then two small containers of milk and a cup for coffee. Ahead of me Fred has filled every corner of his tray and is reaching back for a piece of the same pie, which he places on my tray.

"Hey, Dr. Evers," the cashier says as Fred guides our trays to her station. "Carol know you're seein' other women?"

Fred smiles and introduces me as his "long lost cousin" while he pays for our lunches. We fill our coffee cups at the beverage station and head for a quiet corner. I can still hear the cha-ching of the cash register and the clanking of dishes but we are far enough from the rest of the diners to reduce their conversations to background noise. We unwrap our plastic flatware in silence. I crush my crackers inside the bag then open it and drop the crumbs in my soup. While I stir the soup and crumbs together I watch Fred cut his chicken breast into small pieces and push the cooked carrots to the side of the plate.

"So, Fred," I say opening one of the milk containers and pouring some into my coffee. "Why were you asking Harold Santini about the summer Uncle Ed died?"

Fred slowly takes the paper off his straw and presses it between his finger and thumb. Then pressing with his other thumb and finger he irons the paper flat. Then he carefully folds the straw paper into a tiny square and lays it on the corner of his tray. "You're not going to like this, Molly," he says looking at the paper.

"Why?"

"Because Uncle Ed's death wasn't an accident." He looks up and I can feel my legs shaking. I take a deep breath and try not to choke. "I haven't got all the details worked out, you understand. But something's not right and I'm pretty sure that his death was deliberate."

The soup is suddenly not appealing. I pick up my coffee and hold the mug in front of my face as I ask. "What do you have so far?"

Fred digs in to his lunch and between bites he says. "It was the Matthews case that really made me think about it. Charlene just disappearing like she did, and now being found, after all these years, in the lake. And, you know, I never really understood when Ed died, why they hushed it all up like they did. Aunt Helen took you back down state so you probably didn't hear about it all, but for a couple of years the investigation, or lack of it, was the main topic of conversation at the barbershop, and the diner. Then folks just lost interest, I guess. But you know, I like a good mystery, like finding a buried treasure, so I kept trying to find out things. I mean, I tried to get hold of the autopsy report when I was interning, and they told me it was sealed. So there must be something there, don't you think? I mean, if it was a drowning, why all the secrecy? Molly? Are you all right?"

My hands are shaking. I can feel the blood leaving my face and my muscles going to putty. I put the cup down and hold the edge of the table. Fred leans across the table and grasps my arms. "Molly, my god! You're pale as a ghost. You look like someone just walked over your grave." When he's sure I won't fall out of the chair he lets go of my arms and settles back in his chair.

"Here, eat. I'm sorry Molly, I wasn't thinking. I didn't mean to bring it all up again, I remember how upset you were when Uncle Ed died. God, what was I thinking?" He shakes his head and sighs.

"It's okay," I say, though I am very close to tears. "Really, it's okay."

"Why don't we eat our dessert first?" Fred says, digging his plastic fork into the second piece of pie on my tray. "Some fool always calls me away in the middle of dinner, and I never get to eat my dessert."

"We should always eat our pie first," I agree. I pick up my fork and tackle the other pie.

"Do you remember Howard Santini from the lake?" Fred asks, using the back of his hand to wipe banana cream off his chin.

"No," I admit, and hand him a napkin.

"Neither do I, but don't tell him that. He remembers you, you know. Told me he had a sort of crush on 'that skinny gal that read books while she fished.' That would be you, right?."

I smile a little. A ten year old Freddie Evers could charm the socks off a person. All grown up he was a force to be reckoned with. I worry what he's going to think of me when he learns the truth, but I think that whatever happens Fred will be there for me. "Thank you," I tell him.

"For this paltry lunch, no thanks necessary."

"No, not for lunch."

"Then for what?"

"Just . . . thank you."

A buzzer sounds, sending everyone in our general vicinity searching in pockets and backpacks for their beepers. Fred pulls his out of his jacket pocket and reads the display. "It's me," he says, waving the beeper for the other tables to see. "Got to go Molly, See you at the house, later?"

I watch him walk purposefully across the room and out the door. Many of the other diners are checking their watches or clearing their tables. I sit for a moment wondering if I should leave. I could get in my car and drive back home to Lansing, let Helen take care of the damn cottage. Why am I here? Why don't I run? In the end it's not my desire to escape that wins out, it's that my knees are still weak and I'm not sure I'll make it to the door if I try. Besides I always want to know how a story ends, so I stay. I sip my coffee, and finish the pie. The cashier comes over with the coffee pot and pours me another cup.

"Refills are free honey. Sit as long as you like."

Another lunchroom worker is mopping up tables and as he passes mine he takes away Fred's tray. I dip the plastic spoon in my cold soup and finish that off too. I'm pouring the last of my milk into my third refill of coffee, and scanning the nearly empty room, when two men enter. One is wearing a pale blue sport jacket and white pants and the other, a doctor maybe, has on green surgical scrubs and a surgical cap the color of Yvonne Potter's fingernails. Thinking of Yvonne reminds me of the phone call from Will Campion. I stir my coffee and try to remember his voice, kind of soft and uncertain as he spoke. He was really quoting Fred, of course, "Not like most folks, in a nice way." But it was still nice to hear. Oh, I know, Helen would say. "It's just like you, Molly, making a peach pie from a single pit." But it wasn't the words so much, it was the way Will Campion said them. I close my eyes and try to remember what it sounded like.

"Done with that?"

I open my eyes and lift the coffee cup so the worker can take my tray. Across the room I see the back of the blue sport coat. The man is sitting with his head lowered and the doctor standing beside him has a hand on the man's shoulder. I watch as the doctor walks away and the man in the sport coat leans further over, as if he is inspecting the floor. He begins to cough, a choking kind of cough. I look over to see the lunchroom worker pushing a cart stacked with trays through the doors to the dish room. The cashier is gone too. I wonder if the man is choking on food. Suddenly he bangs on the table. I stand and look around the empty cafeteria, hoping someone will appear, a doctor or nurse maybe. No one. As I hurry across the room, I can almost hear Helen saying "Go get help. Don't do anything yourself, you'll just get into trouble." I'm going to be arrested any moment anyway, so what difference could it make. Maybe a good deed is just what my karma needs. "No good deed goes unpunished," I hear Helen's voice in my head.

"Are you all right?" I ask the when I reach him.

"He looks up and all of the oxygen leaves the room. His eyes, though bloodshot, are intensely blue and his boyish good looks are movie star gorgeous.

"What? What?" he is saying.

I catch my breath, realizing I'm still holding my coffee mug. "I'm sorry, I was over there."

His gaze follows my ineffective gesture across the room to where my purse and package lean on the chair leg.

"Um, there's no one else here, and I, um, thought you needed help. I'm uh, I'm sorry."

"No, no," he says politely. He clears his throat and stands. "I'm Rob. RJ to my friends. Please, sit." He pushes back the chair.

"I, I don't want to intrude, Rob," I say, allowing him to guide me into the chair.

"Please," he says. "Call me RJ, and really, I could use some company." He takes a handkerchief from his back pocket, blows his nose loudly, replaces the kerchief and asks, "What was your name again?"

"Molly. I'm Molly."

"Have we met before, Molly?"

"I don't think so, I'm not from around here."

"Well, you look familiar, anyway. So tell me, what's a nice girl like you doing in a place like this? Somebody sick? Husband, boyfriend maybe?"

I shake my head no and sip my cold coffee. "You?"

He looks down at his coffee, shakes his head slowly and says. "My boy. You got any kids, Molly?"

"No, no kids. Not even a husband, yet." Yeah Helen, I hear you. He's married.

"Well, it's a hard thing, I can tell you. Seeing your child lying there, helpless, hooked up to monitors and machines and knowing there isn't anything at all you can do. The doctors, you know, they tell you all the medical particulars, best case scenarios, worst case scenarios. But, they don't know really. They don't."

"I'm sorry. Is his mother with him now?"

He looks up, arching one eyebrow and says, "his mother?"

"Your wife," I prompt.

"My wife," he says, covering his eyes with his hand for a moment then drawing his finger and thumb together on the bridge of his nose. "My wife left me, it's just me and the kid."

"Oh. I see." Crooked Lake is beginning to look like a single fathers camp. First Will Campion and his boy Billy, then the dead woman's husband that Carol is so mad about and his boy and now this poor guy.

"It was a long time ago. I've almost forgotten about it." He smiles and when he does, the wrinkles at the corners of his eyes deepen and a lock of blond hair slips across his forehead. He reaches up and smooths it back. "So Molly," he says, "You're visiting then? Maybe you and I can go to dinner sometime, what do you think?"

I cup my hands around my coffee mug. He's just asking to be polite, I tell myself. He's not trying to pick me up. This isn't that sweaty handed bookstore clerk surprising me in the reference room, or one of the pathetically horny ex-jocks at the sports bar, trying for a score. "That would be nice," I hear myself say.

"Look, I'm going to be here for most of the day. They're doing some tests. But, well, a body's got to eat, don't they? There's a great Steak & Ale about ten miles north of here.. Local color, intimate atmosphere, and the food's not bad either. What do you say. Sixish? Where are you staying?"

"With my cousin. He has a place on the big lake. You probably know him, he's lived here for years. Fred Evers."

"Sure, I know Fred." For a moment RJ looks puzzled, then he says quickly, "You know, I just remembered a call I have to make. Listen, How about I meet you at the Speckled Trout in Chandler for a drink first, then we'll drive up to the Inn.for dinner? The Speckled Trout, on Main and Turner, sixish? You'll be there?"

"Sure, I'll be there." I watch him cross the room. He walks purposefully, his arms churning and his coattails swinging.

When he reaches the doorway he turns, adjusts his lapels with his thumbs, smiles and nods his head in my direction.

I return to my table for a few more minutes, and sip my cold coffee. Twenty years ago I might have drowned when Uncle Ed threw me into the lake. Was it chance alone that saved me, or a force of will that, at eleven, I was unable to recognize. And what if Uncle Ed had gone with the family to the Shoreline that night instead of taking a load of fireworks and a six pack out onto the lake. Would he be alive now too?

The dull clunk of my cup striking the table echoes through the room. My hand tightens on the handle. If I hadn't sabotaged the boat, spilled the gasoline, hated Uncle Ed so much. . . In the caramel colored residue inside my cup I can almost see a stray spark from a bottle rocket ignite the fuel soaked boards on the boat bottom. I push the cup away and close my eyes against the picture.

What would RJ think of me if he knew ? Would he still want to meet me for dinner at the Speckled Trout if he knew that I killed my Uncle Ed? A sudden picture of Officer Campion, standing at the edge of the land bridge above the submerged car enters my mind. "Sweet Jesus," he is saying.

Sweet Jesus.

12

I'm surprised at how much I remember about Chandler. Oh, it has grown. Twenty years, how could it not? The hospital takes up a whole city block now. But the downtown area is basically the same long street in my childhood memory. I find the register of deeds office in a courthouse annex next to the ice cream parlor, only two blocks from Chandler Realty. I remember it as a new building some twenty five years ago when Cliff helped Gran sign over the family home to Aunt Harriet when Gran and Uncle Ed moved permanently to the cottage. The facade looks old and worn, especially compared to the newly refurbished ice cream parlor, its picket fence decor-plastic made to look like the original, only shiny. I stop to put my ruined jacket in the car when a spurt of laughter directs my attention past the car to a group of women across the street. I notice the sign for the Speckled Trout above them. They wear dresses and high heeled shoes and the men who come out after them wear suits. I open the car door and watch them while I mentally sort through my suitcase and look sadly at the plastic bag of ruined jacket on the car seat. Even if the stains came out, I think as I lock the car door, the jacket won't be wearable tonight. And all I have in my suitcase is more jeans and T's.

The inside of the Annex is a surprise. Unlike the worn and slightly shabby exterior, the halls are well lit and clean and the deeds office is a clearly marked counter to the left of the main door. "Can I help you?" the woman behind the counter asks.

"Yes, I hope so. Apparently my grandmother's name wasn't taken off a property deed when she passed away some years ago. Can you tell me what I have to do?"

"Do you know the property number?

I shrug and offer, "It's a cottage on Crooked Lake Road."

"Big lake, or little?"

"Little."

"Your grandmother's name?"

"Betsy Evers. Well her given name was Elizabeth. It's one of the small cottages on the North Shore."

"Oh, I'm sure I can find that record. Lots of interest in those properties lately. I'll bet I've thumbed those files at least ten times this week. You got some identification? I'll need to see ID. Driver's License will do. Do you have a death certificate?"

"No," I tell her.

"Well, you'll need a copy of the death certificate, in order to take the name off the deed. If she died here abouts you ought to be able to get that at the clerk's office down the hall."Get all the paperwork completed and bring it back Friday. I won't be here tomorrow, got a downstate funeral to go to. Madge'll be here but she'll just screw up all the paperwork and I'll have to unscrew it when I get back, so please just bring it back Friday. Okay?

I nod my head as she goes through a large vault door at the back of the room and then I dig through my wallet for my ID. The clerk leans out from the vault door.

"Say, I think this is the right property. Evers you said? On the little lake?"

"That's right," I say. I hear a drawer on ball bearings rumble and close with a clank, and the clerk returns to counter with a file folder.

"Well, there's only one property that lists an Evers, but it isn't Elizabeth. It's an Edward Lloyd Evers. That be her husband, you think?"

"No that would be her son, my mother's brother. But he died before Gran did. I thought the deed was joint with my mother, Helen Swain. Now what do I do?"

"Well, there's a Swain here, but it ain't Helen. You wouldn't happen to be Molly Irene Swain, would you?"

"As a matter of fact I am."

"Well, this property is titled to you, and to Edward Lloyd Evers. You didn't know?

"No. Helen pays the taxes. I just assumed."

"Oh well, anyone can pay the taxes. As long as they are paid, the county really doesn't get into it. Did Mr. Evers die recently?"

"Oh, no. It's been twenty years. I was just eleven years old."

"Oh sure, that explains it. Helen's your mother right? Probably she was just waiting till you were an adult to transfer it."

"I'm 31!"

"Maybe she forgot."

13

I look over at the pile of papers next to me on the car seat. The stained plastic bag that held my jacket is scrunched on top of several copies of Uncle Ed's death certificate, a quit claim deed application, and a hand written sheet from a legal pad outlining the steps that need to be taken. My linen jacket, wrinkled and stained and not very appealing, slumps across the seat back like a deflated mannequin. Accepting the invitation to dinner was stupid. Why didn't I just say no? I could have said I had plans already, or something. I don't even own anything like what those women downtown were wearing. I imagine several of the outfits hanging in my closet down state. Nothing dressy there either, I'm not much of a clothes horse. Another of Helen's criticisms. I only have the linen jacket because it was a gift from Helen, and it was cool when I left Lansing. Now it's wrinkled and stained and probably even dry cleaning won't save it. I put the car in gear and look into the rear view mirror. The sign for Chloe's, a fashionable boutique stares back at me. Why not? I think, putting the car back into park and grabbing my purse. After all, I just learned I'm a home owner. I should celebrate.

Chloe's in the kind of store I usually avoid. I'm a dedicated discount store shopper. Push around a cart and pick up everything you need from food to underwear, no interruptions. I did try to buy clothes in a mall once, but the clerks kept insisting I "try something on." The idea of changing my clothes in a small booth sent me flying out without a purchase. Luckily, it appears I'm the only customer in the place and this clerk seems content to lets me peruse the racks unaided. I find a denim jacket I like in my size, and a pair of earrings that resemble fish with articulated scales to mimic movement. Most of the dresses are floral, with capped sleeves and revealing necklines, but I find a simple sleeveless dress, kind of a dusty green with a subtle fern-like pattern in it, on the clearance rack. It's a size smaller than I usually wear, but it looks generously cut so I take a chance. I find a pair of white sandals, which are also marked down . The clerk takes her time running my credit card and folding my purchases into tissue covered bundles which she then layers in a handled bag. I feel slightly giddy as I leave the shop, having spent more than a hundred dollars on clothes. I let the car idle a few minutes while I breathe deeply and look uncertainly at my purchases, then head for Fred's place.

I see Billy Campion squeezed into a corner of the back porch when I pull the car into the drive. If not for the thin arms pulling his baggy-jean clad legs tightly to his chest and the small sad face under the bill of his baseball cap, I could easily mistake him for a pile of old clothes.

"Hi Billy," I say, walking past him to the door. He sits stone faced and silent, and I feel bad when I open the screen door and leave him alone with the mismatched cushions and faded wicker chairs on the Evers kitchen porch. Carol looks up from a partially rolled pie crust and rubs her nose with the back of one flour coated hand. I question her with a frown and a nod towards the bundled figure on the porch.

"He's been like that all day," she tells me, sprinkling flour across a wooden rolling pin and pushing it deftly across the dough. I stand by the door and watch her fold the circle of dough in half over the rolling pin, pick it up and lay it expertly across half of a large ceramic pie plate. She frowns slightly as she draws the top half of the dough across the bare half of the dish and pats it gently into the dish's contours. "The girls tried to get him to play," she says, looking up briefly before picking up a paring knife and dipping the blade into a glass of water. She holds the knife against the edge of the plate and turns the plate slowly to pare away the excess crust. "He's not eating either. I made the kids pizza for lunch and he just sat there nibbling the edges. My girls act out when they're hurting, you know. I know how to deal with that. But Billy, he's all drawn inside himself, like a basketball bug."

I look through the window at the boy, his face turned down now and the bill of the ball cap partially covering his tightly squeezed knees. A basketball bug. I remember basketball bugs. Turning over rocks by the roadside after a rain, watching the oddly sectioned brown bugs turn themselves into tiny basketballs to escape my ever-prying curiosity. The more I poked and prodded the tighter those stubborn little bugs curled up.

"Strawberry rhubarb is his favorite pie," Carol says, pouring a mixture of purple and red into the freshly made crust. "His mother gave me this recipe before she died, but I don't think it's going to help."

"When did she die?" I ask. I shrug my purse strap off my shoulder and put it with my papers and bag on the counter.

"Laurie? Oh, I don't know." She begins laying strips of dough, like lattice, across the pie. "Let's see, Fred had just got promoted to the M.E. job when Julie died. Ectopic pregnancy. Totally out of the blue. I guess that'd make it six years ago or so. Why?"

"Oh, just curious. Does he remember her?"

"I doubt it," Carol says. She lays the last strip of dough across the pie and pinches off the excess. "He was very young, not even in school yet. And Will says he never talks about her."

Doesn't mean he doesn't think about her, I tell myself. I leave my things where I dropped them on the counter and step back through the door to the porch. "Mind if I sit out here with you?" I ask Billy.

He shrugs and emits a sharp sigh. The cushions wheeze as I settle into them, and the old wicker chair squeaks when I lean back and close my eyes. In the kitchen the oven door groans a protest at opening and bangs shut on the unbaked pie. Carol begins to hum as she winds an antique timer and sets it on the counter. The hum dissolves into an off key rendition of "Got the whole world in my hands" as she stacks the mixing bowls and dishes in the sink.

I open my eyes to see a crooked smirk under the bill of the boy's cap. He looks up suddenly and our eyes meet. I laugh, and still smiling, close my eyes again. He isn't completely gone, I assure myself. I saw a sparkle in those beautiful brown eyes, like a shiny copper penny on the lake bottom, revealed only when the lake is still and the light is just right, and even then only someone searching will see it. I was that penny once myself, looking up through the weed infested murk of childhood, struggling to find myself in the quick sand of the Evers genealogical chart. Cliff saw me, when no one else, not even Helen, did. And then Cliff was gone, and when Uncle Ed threw me into the lake, Cliff wasn't there to save me. And when I killed Uncle Ed, Cliff wasn't there to tell. So I locked up the evidence in Gran's candy tin and buried it. Someone is bound to find it soon and make the connection. Before they do I feel a curious need to reach into the depths and bring the sparkling penny that is Billy Campion to the surface. Don't poke I remind myself, or he'll roll up like the basketball bugs. I settle myself deeper in the cushions and let out a long sigh.

Carol's discordant melody recedes as her domestic chores take her deeper into the old house. A few bird like chirrups and an occasional cricket, sawing, disturbs the calm. The warm afternoon breeze massages the day from our minds, as the silence on the porch prepares to engulf us.

While I sleep the Evers dog, apparently bored with frisbee chasing or watching minnows off the dock with Fred's girls, sprawls on the cool concrete at my feet. His tail thumping joyfully at the arrival of his master wakes me. Fred is climbing out of his SUV in the drive. Long shadows sprawl into the yard and my bare arms are goose pimpled. I rub them and myself awake. Billy is curled around a large floral pillow on the window settee at the far end of the porch. His ball cap has fallen to the floor and his dark hair spills across his forehead and onto the pillow. He is really a younger version of his father. Dark eyes and hair, strong but vaguely feminine hands. Vulnerable mouth.

"So, Molly," Fred says leaning over to rub the dog's upturned belly. "Sorry I didn't get back to you at the hospital. Another accident over at the new canal site. Damn near lost a man. That idiot Matthews is going to kill somebody one of these days. Oh hey, ran into Yvonne Cooper while I was there. Said you had to get some title work done on the old cottage. Find everything okay?"

Billy stirs on the settee. "Shhhh," I tell Fred as I untangle myself from the dog at my feet. A strong smell of rhubarb apple pie and pot roast fills the air. I get up from the chair and motion for Fred to follow me into the house. Carol is busy setting up the table for dinner. She hands Fred a stack of plates. "Dinner's just about ready," she hollers out the window to her girls. Fred walks around the table, placing plates on place mats, and doesn't look surprised when I tell him the cottage was titled to Uncle Ed, and me.

"It figures," he says, gesturing with the last plate. "Gran gave the homestead to my mother, to carry on the Evers traditions, me being the last male in the Evers line. Course we had a fire my senior year in high school, so the old Evers homestead is gone. I remember though, my mother saying they bought the cottage with Uncle Ed's separation money from the army."

Carol hands me a basket of flatware and I follow Fred's lead around the table, placing the knives and forks next to the plates. "But why would Uncle Ed put my name on it?"

"You got me there," Fred says. "Unless they just wanted to make sure it went to the next generation, and you and I are it. I'm told Aunt Helen made it very clear she didn't want anything to do with the place." Charlene and Frieda stumble through the door carrying their fishing poles and worm buckets. "Wash up!" Fred tells them.

"You too, Fred!" Carol places a large covered pot on a cork mat in the center of the table and turns to look directly at Fred. "Heaven only knows where those hands have been. Now git."

Fred winks at me and heads for the staircase. He turns before the first step and asks, "What are we having, anyway?"

"Roast," she tells him. "We would have had a beautiful speckled trout, but the girls got excited and tried to reel him in too fast."

"Trout!" I blurt looking down at my watch. It's ten till six. "Oh my god, I'm late!"

Fred and Carol are looking at me, waiting for an explanation.

"I have a date at the Speckled Trout in Chandler," I say, picking up my things from the counter.

"Well, cousin, you work fast. Who's the lucky guy?"

"Someone I met at the hospital," I tell Fred, hurrying past him up the stairs.

I manage a quick once over with a wash rag and pull my hair back into a clip. The new earrings and some lipstick make me presentable. I pass a smiling Fred in the hall. After I shake out the wrinkles and remove the tags from my purchase I discard my jeans and T and slip my new dress over my head. It fits rather nicely, maybe even a little loose. I dump the shoe box upside down and slide my bare feet into the new sandals. I can't believe I'm dressing up for a date, I'm even a little nervous.

Carol's voice from the hall way echoes, "It's supposed to get down to the 50's tonight, so you might need a jacket."

"Thanks," I tell her as she peeks in at the doorway. "Do you think this will do?."

I put the new denim jacket in front of me and kick out the skirt of the dress a little.

"It's lovely," Carol says. "And I'm so glad you are going on a date. You deserve to have a little fun while you're here. Lord knows you stepped into a rat's nest when you arrived. Go out and paint the town red!."

We hug and Carol leaves me to assess my outfit. "Paint the town" was one of Gran's favorite sayings, though I'd never heard anyone say what color to paint it till now. The dress is something I'm not used to. I like a skirt that touches my ankles, better yet pants, and this dress barely covers my knees. The sandals fit perfectly though and I hope are appropriate attire for the Trout. I pull the tiny chain from it's secret compartment and my wallet becomes a very small purse. The whole family looks up when I hurry down the stairs holding the jacket and wallet/purse in one hand.

"You look lovely," Carol says. The girls shake their heads in approval, without missing a bite. Billy looks up and almost smiles, then looks quickly back at his plate. "Molly," Fred says. "You clean up right nice. Hope this fella you're going out with knows a good thing when he sees it."

"Thanks," I say and hurry out the door.

14

"Thought maybe you got a better offer," he says as I turn the corner onto Main St, just remembering to turn and push the lock button on my keychain. He's wearing a knit golf shirt and a sport coat. and leaning against the brick wall, like an advertisement in a magazine.

"Sorry," I hear myself say.

"That's all right," he laughs. "The wait was worth it."

I'm suddenly conscious of my bare legs and tiny sandals.

"Looks like the Trout's a little crowded. Let's have our drinks with dinner, eh."

I look past him at a line of about 20 people at the door of the Grill. "Wow," I say "and on a week night too."

"Tourists," he says. "Come on." He pushes himself off the wall and takes my hand. "You're gonna love the Inn.," he says as he opens the door of the Lincoln and helps me inside. The car engine is silent as we back out of the parking space and float gently down the street. The leather seat is incredibly soft. I sink into it relaxing into the warm comfort.

"Heated seats," RJ says, turning onto the highway and accelerating into the light traffic.

"What?" I say, looking past him at the forested landscape.

"The seats," he says. "They're heated. I know it sounds crazy, being as it's summer. But you know the tinted windows keep the sun out and I find if I just heat the seats a little, it makes the car really comfortable. You like my car?"

"It's lovely," I tell him." And it is.

"Got a really good deal, too. Guy over in Petoskey got in over his head and had to liquidate. He wanted forty grand, but he was desperate so I got it for thirty. It's got a few years on it, but, you know these aren't your normal off the line boxes. Not much call for them up here, either. Oh maybe over in TC, but up this way it's mostly SUVs and Four Wheelers."

"So, tell me about the restaurant."

"Oh, you're gonna love it. It was an Inn, you know like a hotel back in the 40's and 50's. Then it was a corporate retreat for executives and their big clients. I don't know what happened to the corporation, but for nearly ten years it just sat there. Forest fire about got it in the late 90's and then this fella from downstate bought it. Retired fella, says his folks brought him up here when it was an Inn. So anyway, he's rehabbing the place. You know making it look like the 50's but with all the modern amenities. Got the restaurant pretty much done last month. Only been open for business a couple of days, so it might be a little informal yet."

"It sounds lovely," I say. And it really is. We park in a gravel lot and walk up a stone path through a small pine forest. The Inn is nestled in the woods, tall pines obscuring the actual size of the building. The facade reminds me of Gran's cottage. My cottage. The main doors are offset under an irregularly sloped roof, that open to a wide wood paneled hallway. The entry hall is centered between two open staircases, their half log treads still covered in bark where the underside is visible. While RJ speaks with the hostess I gape at the shaved branches, held in iron eye hooks that are pegged into upright beams like tree trunks, weaving a crooked railing up the stairway. Nothing like this downstate. Even the round tiles in the floor are wooden. I can see the tree rings in the cross sections under my feet and remnants of bark still clinging to their edges encased in some darkly transparent grout.

The relatively low ceiling of the entry hall continues in the dining room, where half round logs protrude from the rough plaster ceilings. We settle into a booth near the windows and survey the small number of other diners in the large room.

"So, what does Molly Swain do?" RJ asks, looking over the top of the oversized menu.

"I write." I tell him, laying my own menu on the table in front of me. "I'm a writer." Half truth. I write, but it's not like I'm really a writer.

"Really?" he says. "What do you write, Molly Swain?"

"Nothing anyone has read, I'm afraid. I do some copy writing for a catalog company, do feature stories and interviews for a couple of non-profits. That sort of thing. I did have a short story published, once. In a tiny literary magazine. Very tiny."

"Doesn't sound like a very lucrative occupation, Miss Swain. Does writing pay much?"

"No, not very much."

"So, how do you keep body and soul together? Are you independently wealthy? I'm sorry, is that improper? Should I be asking a woman on a first date how she makes a living? Forget I asked."

"No, it's okay, really. It just doesn't come up that often. I administer a trust."

"Really? Well, that sounds exciting."

"Well, it's not, most of the time. It's mostly paperwork and legal stuff. It's an endowment, so I pretty much just work with the income. Authorize charitable donations and that kind of thing."

"So it's a sizable endowment, huh? You must be a pretty good accountant. How'd you get a job like that."

"My father was the trustee, and he died."

"Oh, I'm sorry. So it's family money, eh?"

The waiter smiles as he pours red wine in our glasses and RJ orders for both of us.

The wine warms me and the food is divine. The room is about half full now and the light hum of the other diners in the background is almost like music. RJ makes casual conversation out of descriptions of the old inn and stories about it's history. I feel like I'm in a movie scene so when RJ lifts a forkful of his pasta bajoul and says, "You've got to try this, Molly," I let him gently guide it into my mouth. It is spicy and sweet at the same time and he watches me chew as if it were crucial that I love it.

"Wonderful," I tell him.

"I knew you would like it!" he exclaims. "I knew it!"

He orders coffee and dessert for us. Normally I like to order for myself, but his choice for dinner was excellent and the wine has blurred more than my vision and it seems somehow natural to let him continue. When we finish he leans back in his chair and places both hands on the table in front of him.

"Well, Molly," he says. "I'm impressed.You're beautiful and smart too. A writer and trust administrator. Your family must be very proud of your accomplishments. You're mother is still living I believe?"

"I doubt it. Oh, I mean, yes she's still living. But I doubt that she's all that proud. I mean it's not like the trust is something I earned. I sort of inherited it."

"Nothing wrong with that, I inherited my first business. Surely she can see how important it is and how well you do it."

"Maybe, but mostly I think she wants me to get married and give her grandchildren." I can't believe I'm talking like this to a man I barely know.

R. A. HANKINS

"Is that a fact? So, tell me Molly, why is a beautiful, accomplished woman like yourself still single?"

Hie eyes are so blue. Accomplished? It's not at all how I think of myself. Beautiful? He thinks I'm beautiful? Why aren't I married? Timing? Luck - or lack of it? Haven't met the right guy yet? Or have I?

"Molly?"

"Hmm?"

"Where were you just now?"

"Oh, I'm sorry. I, I must be tired." Or maybe I've had a little too much wine.

"It is late. I should get you back to Chandler. Can we do this again, Molly? Maybe tomorrow? Say a little earlier - like five'ish? I'll be with my son most of the day, but the Trout doesn't get busy till after 6. I'd sure like to see you again, Molly."

"That would be nice." I tell him.

"The trout at five then?"

"I'll be there!"

We say goodnight under the streetlamp near my car. No awkward first date kiss, he just squeezes my hand and walks away. The night is clear and I drive with the window down to feel the air rushing past. Only the back porch light is on at Fred's when I arrive. I take off my sandals and tiptoe into the house and up the stairs. Alone in the dark I replay tasting the pasta bajoul listen to the echoes of "accomplished," "beautiful."

It's not till daylight that the old insecurities sneak back in.

16

"Hey Molly," Carol calls out from the kitchen as I descend the stairs. "Coffee's ready."

I take a mug of steaming coffee and sit down at the table across from her. She is cleaning paint brushes with a cotton rag and a jar of clear liquid.

"Well," she says, laying the brushes like silverware in a line on an old newspaper.

I shrug my shoulders slightly and take a sip of the too-hot coffee.

"Come on, how was your date? What's he like? Tell me all about it."

"I had a lovely time," I tell her. "We ate at a small inn that's being renovated. I'm not really sure where it is."

"Oh, you went to Riley's. I didn't know he was open yet."

"Well, the food is great. You and Fred should go there."

"Molly, you know I don't want to know about the food. Tell me about your date. Is he a doctor? What's his name? Maybe I know him."

"Well, he's very handsome. And he's divorced I think."

"You think? You mean you went out with a man who might be married?"

"No, He's not married. It's just that, well. The thing is we mostly talked about me."

"Well, that's a good sign, I guess." Carol fingers the brushes, moving them slightly farther apart on the paper. "Most men talk your ear off and it's all about them. So who is he anyway? Is it serious?"

"Well, it was only the first date," I tell her. I can't tell her I don't even know his last name. "I do like him. He seems really nice. We have another date tonight. Are you getting ready to paint?"

"Oh no. I just thought these needed some refreshing."

"I saw you pieces in the den. You're very good. Do you sell many?"

"I did. We used to have a small gallery in Chandler. The owner was a retired art teacher - but I guess she wasn't making enough so she quit and went back downstate. I don't think she had much of a head for business, you know, but she was a lot of fun. Now I have a couple of pieces at the library and I've got a couple of pieces to take to Chloe's this afternoon, for her window display. The summer crowd seems to like them."

The mention of the dress shop reminds me I have another date and nothing to wear.

"Why don't you come with me?" Carol asks. "I'm going to drop the girls at the school. Billy even said he'd go. Summer rec is doing an afternoon movie marathon. I have a few errands, then we could have lunch in town and I could drop off the pictures before I pick up the kids."

So we drop Billy and the girls off at the school and have a nice lunch at a small diner in Cascade. We order from the hand written menu on a blackboard perched in the arms of the restaurant's namesake, a large black bear carved from a tree trunk. The Bear Paw is both cheerful and homey. The knotty pine walls are adorned with pictures of dancing bears. Carol tells me the quilt hanging on the wall is a bear-paw pattern.

We both order chicken strips and fries and Carol only smiles when I ask for mustard instead of catsup for my fries.

"So, Molly, she says as she unwinds her napkin from her flatware. "Tell me more about your mystery man. Is he really good looking?"

"He is," I admit. "Think Don Johnson in Miami Vice."

"Oh really, so where is "Sonny" taking you tonight?"

"The Speckled Trout."

"Oh."

"What?"

"Oh it's nothing. It's just that the Trout is so uppity at night. It's okay during the day, you know when the lights are up and it's not full of posers and all. But after five they yuppie it up. You know, down the lights, double the prices. The class of the clientele goes down too."

"I'm meeting him at five."

"Oh for Heavens sake! Don't pay any attention to me, Molly. I'm just an opinionated old married lady. Nothing wrong with the Trout. It's just that Chandler is changing so much. It's not the small town it was when I grew up here."

We're both quiet on the ride from Cascade to Chandler. At Chloe's I help Carol carry in the pictures. They are all like the ones in her den. She and Chloe begin arranging them among the purses and scarves in the display window. I head for the sale racks and look for my size. The dresses are all flouncy and not my style so I begin looking at the slacks and tops. I find a nice pair of khacki slacks and a long tank top in off white. "Oh, I like those," Carol says walking past me to the back of the store. She pulls a small easel from behind a rack and heads up the aisle with it. "Go ahead and try them on, it's right there." She points to a small changing room with a chair and mirror. I look around the empty store and decide, just this one time to try on clothes in a store. I pull the curtain closed and take several deep breaths. I'm surprised at how nicely the clothes fit me and how different nice clothes make me feel. I turn and look over my shoulder to see it from the back, pull at the shoulders and let the silky fabric drop back into place.I step out of the room to find Carol and Chloe finished with their window dressing.

"You look stunning," Carol tells me.

"Stunning," Chloe echoes. "And I have the most beautiful cardigan that would go perfectly with that outfit." She strides to the front of the shop, pulls a teal sweater/jacket off a rack and strides back. "You simply must try it." she croons.

Carol nods and they both help me try on the cardigan. It's an extra long jacket, an inch or so longer than the tank. I look at my reflection in the mirror and think for a moment that someone else has come into the store. "Do you think it's me?" I ask Carol.

"Are you kidding?" she laughs. "You look fabulous. This poor schnook you're going out with doesn't have a chance."

Chloe wraps my purchases in tissue and layers them in the bag. I find a long scarf with the same blue as the cardigan as I wait for her to ring up the sale. I pay with my credit card and Carol and I leave to pick up Billy and the girls. It isn't till Carol pulls into traffic that I look at the receipt and realize I have spent another hundred and fifty dollars. Helen would be proud.

17

The tiny entry of the Speckled Trout swallows all trace of the warm afternoon. It might as well be midnight inside. Votive candles in colorful fish-shaped bowls barely illuminate the ridiculously small tables in the dining room beyond, much less those seated at them. I pull on the new cardigan, as cold air blasts from an overhead duct, and find the price tags which I forgot to remove. The noise level indicates a crowd.

"I'm meeting someone," I tell the hostess, my eyes attempting to adjust to the sudden darkness, my hands wrestling the tags out of sight, up the sleeve.

"Reservation?" the hostess asks.

"I don't know. I suppose he might have made a reservation."

"Name?" the hostess asks, almost rolling her eyes. I suppose she thinks I can't see her. Name? I look past the hostess where the glowing candles illuminate disembodied hands lifting forks or glasses and disappearing into the darkness, hoping to see RJ's baby blue sport coat. Helen's reproving voice lingers in my subconscious.

"Your name?" Her smile tightens.

"Swain, I'm Molly Swain."

"Ah," the hostess breathes. A click of her fingers brings a young man in crisp black trousers and a starched white shirt. I follow him through the sea of tables and sit in the chair he offers. Across the small table is an empty chair although a glass of half melted ice sits on a soggy coaster near the orange fish bowl. The table is under another cold air duct, I pull the sweater tighter and fumble with the buttons.

"Can I get you a cocktail?" the young man asks, scooping up the glass and coaster, and wiping the table with a white towel.

"Do you have lemonade?" I ask.

"Of course," he replies. "One lemonade coming up."

As soon as he leaves I wish I'd ordered hot chocolate. I try to pull the tags loose from the sleeve but they are firmly attached. I push them back up the sleeve and hope no one notices. The fish bowl candle flickers in the draft and I concentrate on the ghastly pink aura it makes on my hands until the waiter arrives with my lemonade. Then I hold the glass firmly and try to look casually around the room. Light spills from the kitchen as waiters emerge with trays or return with stacks of dishes. I begin to see variations in the dark shadows around me. Shapes begin to emerge from the darkness. The hum of conversation evolves into discernible words at the tables closest to mine. A glint of metal draws my glance toward the ceiling, where an old catch net dangles from a worn cork handle. To the right of the net hang several lures and a large stuffed fish is suspended above them, as if ready to strike. I concentrate on the dark shadow above the net, which appears to extend for several feet. The shape is familiar. Coffin like. Icy air washes across my upturned face. I swallow hard and resist the urge to run.

"Miss Swain," a voice draws me back to the orange glow of the candlelight.

"We met the other day," the voice urges. "At the hospital."

"Mr. Santini," I say looking into the hopeful face of the hospital administrator, glowing pink in the candle light.

"Call me Howard, please." he says.

"Howard." I smile, thinking again how much he reminds me of a puppy.

"Are you alone?" He puts his hand on the back of the empty chair.

"Well, I'm meeting someone."

"Oh," he says. "I-I won't keep you then. Good to see you again. . . Molly."

I watch as he blends back into the darkness and try to remember him from twenty years ago on Crooked Lake. I was so absorbed in books and staying out of the way, I can't remember a single child from those summers. Except Fred, of course.

"I thought you were going to stand me up." The voice and the powder blue jacket penetrate the darkness at the same time although the light makes the jacket look lavender. "I'm really glad you didn't."

"I lost track of the time," I admit, fingering the coaster edge, and noticing that my teal cardigan looks almost pink.

"Yeah," he says. "That happens here. I think it's the lake air."

I sip lemonade and try to think of something to say. The young waiter returns, bringing RJ a fresh coaster and a short glass filled with amber liquid and ice. He takes a quick sip.

"So, Molly. You're here to sell some lakefront property, right?"

"How did you know that?" I ask.

"Yvonne Potter, poor thing." He leans toward the table and says in a more subdued voice, "She thinks you're trying to steal her man."

"She told you that?"

"Well, with Yvonne, reading between the lines isn't very hard. She's been working on that poor deputy for years. Ever since his wife passed away. And just when she thinks she's got him cornered, well . . . anyway she's got a bee in her bonnet about you and him. Any truth to that, Molly? I mean, have I got any chance at all?" The flickering candle light obscures his face and his intense blue eyes tell me nothing.

"I barely know Officer Campion," I say. "He answered the nine-one-one call when I found the boys. You know the ones who hit the submerged car in the big lake. One of them was his son, Billy."

"That was you?"

"Yeah." I take a long sip of lemonade, and close my eyes against the scene. I hear the clink of ice against glass, and the dull clunk of the glass against the coaster, then a long silence. I open my eyes.

"It must have been awful," RJ reaches across the table and covers my hand with his. "Just awful."

I nod. His hand is warm and strong. He reminds me of Cliff. Cliff taking my tiny child hand in his, leading me into a classroom for the first time. It was never Helen, always Cliff holding my hand, giving me strength to do some new thing. Cliff, who took me on my first ferris wheel ride, to my first scary movie, on my first airplane trip.

"Listen," he says, squeezing my hand. "Let's get out of here. I need a little of that lake air, I think." He drops a few bills next to his empty glass and we wind our way through the tables toward the door. He's still holding my hand.

"Have a good evening sir," the young waiter call after us. RJ turns, pulling me with him to give a short wave to the waiter. A brief splinter of light snakes from the kitchen doorway and reveals the long underside of an old wooden rowboat nailed to the ceiling, where moments ago I imagined a coffin. From the entryway the rowboat's outline is unmistakable.

My cold shiver is soon erased by the warm afternoon sun as we stroll silently with other walkers past the shopfronts of

Chandler. I admire Carol's paintings in Chloe's window, am struck by how the soft folds of colorful scarves and textures of straw purses add to the pictures appeal. We pass my car and I notice how the teal of my cardigan and the blue of his jacket dissolve together and then part into blocks of color on the reflective door panel as we pass. The shopping district ends with the sidewalk and he turns to me and says, "Are you hungry?"

"Famished," I admit.

Well, there's an Italian place over in Alanson, and a BBQ out by the highway. What sounds good to you?"

"How about here?" We are standing in the light of a neon sign announcing the "Burger Palace." The building is a short walk lakeside, and we sit at a red painted picnic table to eat greasy burgers and corrugated french fries and stare out at the water. The air is warm, and we talk about the weather and the burgers. This is as relaxed as I have ever been with a man.

"So, Molly, What do you think of our little village? Oh that's right. Yvonne said you used to live here.."

"No, I just came here summers to visit," I say. "A long time ago. In fact this is my first trip back since I was eleven."

"Really? What happened when you were eleven?" he asks, then takes a bite of burger.

"It was a horrible year. Really horrible. Cliff, he was my stepfather, he died, suddenly, just before our annual visit to Gramma Evers'. Helen, my mother, went a little crazy and then my Uncle Ed died in a boating accident. You might have heard about it." I take a big bite of my burger and hope he changes the subject.

"Ed Evers? The guy who did the fire works display and the boat caught fire and burned. That was your Uncle?"

"Yeah." I say, still chewing. I stare at the french fry I am dangling above the spot of mustard on the paper basket and ask. "What about you?"

"Me?"

"Yeah, how long have you lived here and what do you do?" I bite of the end of the french fry and look into those intense blue eyes. He smiles.

"Oh, I've lived in Chandler my whole life. Played football in high school, went to work washing cars at the Chevrolet Dealership while I was still in school. Today I own the place. Oh, I dabble in other things, got some investments and I'm working on a real estate thing, but the dealership, that's my baby. Chandler Chevrolet, Matthews and Son, if we can't make the deal - you can't be dealt with."

"Oh, are you related to Bobby Matthews?" I ask. Matthews is a fairly common name. Still, I stiffen waiting for his reply.

"No." He smiles, and my shoulders relax. "I am Bobby Matthews, but nobody calls me Bobby anymore." He looks up and sees the question before I ask it. " Yes, it's my boy that was hurt. I should have known it was that Campion kid with him. Always doing risky things that boy. You'd think what with his dad being a police officer he'd be more responsible."

"I'm so sorry," I say. This isn't the man Carol described. I watch as he puts down the burger and wipes his hands on a paper napkin. His eyes water, but no tears run down his cheeks.

"I know," he says. "Everybody is."

"How is he doing, your boy?"

"The doctors won't give me anything definite. But my Kyle, he's a fighter. I want to be there, you know, help him through it, but they told me to go home. There was nothing I could do but wait. It's hard, you know. Waiting. I can't just sit there, watching a machine make him breathe. I can't just sit there, doing nothing. They'll call me if there are any changes. He's all I have." He turns to face the lake and clears his throat.

The burger and fries and the red painted picnic table have suddenly lost their charm. I'm sitting with a man Carol thinks killed his own wife. Could he? I look closely at the laugh lines around his eyes, follow the curve of his cheek and remember my face in the bathroom mirror. I don't look like a murderer either.

"Then the woman in the car in the lake, that was your wife?"

"What?" He turns suddenly and says again, "What?"

"The submerged car, the mustang. That was your wife's car?"

"Oh, God." RJ slumps on the bench and drops his head into his hands on the table top. "Oh my God."

"I'm sorry." I say, reaching across the table and touching his hand. "I thought you knew. I thought they told you. I'm so sorry." For a moment we just sit, silently. His face in his hands, my hand touching his.

"Charlene," he says, finally lifting his head. "Charlene was, unpredictable. We were just kids when we married, of course. We had a little house in Cascade, never had enough money, but we were happy, I thought. Then after the baby, after Kyle was born, she changed. She got depressed. Started drinking. Had fits of anger. Started making up stories, you know? Telling people I hit her, things like that. She'd leave me for a day or two. Then when she was over it, she'd beg me to take her back, and of course I did. I loved her." His lower lip trembles but his eyes are dry. "And now, I know, she's not ever coming back."

"I'm sorry."

"No, it's a relief, really it is."

"Maybe I should go," I say.

"Oh," he says. "No, really. I need a few minutes to process this. Will you walk with me? I really don't want to be alone, just now."

We drop the remains of our dinner into the waste can by the table and walk together to the lake shore behind the

Palace. We stand on a small dock watching the sunlight splinter orange on the water as it descends behind the trees on the opposite shore. We just stand there, watching the darkness overtake the day.

"Sometimes I wish I could just rewind the past," he says. "You know, start over. I wish I could go to sleep tonight and wake up in the morning and start all over. You know what I mean?"

"Yeah." Do I ever. But I know that you can never really start over. You always have the past. In my case the hook, tugging at my consciousness.

He turns his back to the lake and looks up and down the shore. "This was a real happening place once," he says. "Friday night dances at the Anchor Bar, movies at the Lake Theatre. It's all gone now."

He faces the lake again. "When I was a kid, there was a diving float right out there." He points to an imaginary spot on the lake. "You know, a bunch of barrels tied together with a wooden deck on top. Couple of boat anchors to keep it from drifting.

"I think I remember that," I say, surprised by a Crooked Lake memory that isn't painful.

"Yeah. When we were all in high school, Charlie Bauer planted a palm tree on it. His dad was a window dresser and Charlie stole the palm on a dare. He took it out in a rowboat and declared the float an 'island.' Took a keg of beer too, as I remember it. Good old Charlie. Did community service his whole senior year for that one. You know he's Mayor of Chandler now."

"Overcame his youthful indiscretions, I take it."

"Well, he still drinks."

"What ever happened to the float?"

"Oh, eventually some of the barrels rusted out, got filled with water and whole platform tipped over. They opened up the remaining barrels and let the whole thing sink to the bottom. I think that's where I got the idea."

"What idea?"

"Huh?"

"You were saying you got an idea from the old float."

"Oh. Yeah." He looked at me oddly for a moment then said, "For the development. North Shore. I told you I had some real estate deals, didn't I? I'm building a resort, a kind of Club Med, Northern Michigan style. Hey, I'm having some investors out at the site, for cocktails and swimming this weekend. Want to come?"

"Thanks, but I don't swim," I tell him, pulling my cardigan over the goose bumps on my neck, the price tag in the sleeve scraping my arm.

18

Fred's neighbors are having a party. Cars are badly parked on the shoulder of both sides of the road. Fred's drive is partially blocked. I park several houses away and pick my way up the bricked path beside the Evers' house, careful not to trip on any bicycles or frisbees the girls have left out. Just before I reach the back corner of the house a loud bang makes me turn toward the party house, and a burst of bottle rockets shower the sky. I am watching the fireworks as I round the corner and I don't see Officer Campion until we collide. I go down like a pyramid of canned peas at the grocery. Arms flying, knees knocking, ankles bending.

"Ow!" I shout.

Officer Campion, who doesn't fall, leans down and extends his arm. "Are you okay? I didn't see you.'

I take his hand and he hoists me up." Ow!!" I say again. I can't put my weight on my right ankle. I lean into Campion and he manages not to fall over.

"Think you can make it to the beach?" he asks.

"Why? You want to finish the job." I am sorry the minute the words hit the air, but I can't think of any way to get my foot out of my mouth.

"Old indian trick, Campion says. "Put your foot in the water and it won't swell up."

"Really?" With his help I hobble to the beach. He helps me take off my sandals and roll up my pant legs. I sit on the dock edge with both feet in the water. It's cold. But my ankle immediately feels better. "Clever old indian," I say, trying not to let my teeth chatter.

"Indian Scout Will Campion, at your service, ma'am," he says. He sits cross legged beside me.

"What are you doing here, anyway?" I ask.

"Checking on Billy."

"How is he doing?"

"It's hard. He's really not over losing Laurie, and that was six years ago. Laurie was his mother," he says.

"Carol told me, I'm sorry." I kick the water a little and he puts his hand on my knee, forcing my foot back into the water.

"Not yet," he says. I let my legs relax, and he withdraws his hand, slowly.

"It must be hard, raising him alone," I say.

"We do okay." He straightens his back and exhales hard. "My folks live in Iowa, but Laurie's mom helped out for awhile. Till she moved to Florida last year. Sitters haven't worked out, but Billy's almost twelve. We make do."

"You must both miss her."

"Yeah, She used to sing Billy to sleep. That John Denver song. You know, about West Virginia. He asked me to sing it to him tonight, but I can't remember it."

"Oh," I say. "That explains it."

"Explains what?" He looks at me and I can see Billy in the way he holds his head.

"Why he wouldn't let go of me. When I found him, remember? Before the paramedics arrived. He was shivering and crying and I was trying to make him feel better. I held him and the only song I could think of was "Country Roads.""

He looks at me blankly.

"That John Denver song about West Virginia."

"Okay. I think you can walk it off now." he says, pushing himself up from the dock. He helps me up and takes my arm. We walk to the end of the L-shaped dock where Fred's pontoon is still mired in the mud. The pontoons poking out of the water remind me of my hidden box and the men with the metal detectors.

"How's the investigation going?" I ask.

"Can't talk about it."

"Of course. Sorry."

I roll my pant legs down and we turn and walk back to the shore and then down the beach where the wet sand cushions my feet."

"Got the window fixed. The one at your cottage."

"Thanks."

"I did some work on the door frame too. Hope you don't mind."

"No, I don't mind. Thanks."

"It's a nice cottage," he says. "Could use a little TLC."

I shake my head.

"You're going to sell it then?"

"I guess so."

"Too bad. I hate to see it go like the rest. Matthews is going to ruin the Cascade."

"What is he doing?" We turn and walk back toward the dock. My ankle feels almost normal.

"You know about North Shore, right?"

"Not a lot."

"Well, Matthews wants to make money. That's the root of it. He's got his dealership mortgaged to the hilt and he's buying up all the little cottages around the north shore. Yours is one of them. I think he already owns most of the property between the north shore and Cascade, and he's got plans for all of it. Expensive condos, a fancy hotel. And that's just for starters. He's planning an amusement park that'll make Cedar Point look like a church carnival. I know, I've seen the plans."

"Is that bad?" I ask, thinking about the abandoned rentals on the lake. The look he gives me could wither steel beams.

"Listen, Bobby Matthew's "investors" can't wait for the lock to descend and now the lock is unusable. That affects the people who live here, who have business here. He can't wait for an environmental study so he muscles a waiver then excavates a channel. Again the local economy suffers. I hold him personally responsible for the drop in water level on the big lake. Oh, yeah, then he magnanimously "helps" the local economy by buying them out for pennies on the dollar. Folks who've lived their whole lives in Cascade won't be able to afford to live there anymore if Matthew's gets his way. I think that's bad, what do you think?"

"I don't know what to think."

"Well, you can bet it isn't going to get any better? A few years back one of Matthews other businesses was deep in red ink. It burned down, under mysterious circumstances, and he got a bundle from the insurance."

"Couldn't be coincidence?"

"Could be." He says, with a grimace. "But I don't think so."

We stop walking and he looks up at the house. The kitchen light is on.

"Are they waiting up for me?"

"Fred is," he tells me and holds out my sandals.

"Why?" I ask, taking them.

"It's not my business," he says. "I just came by to check on Billy."

"Oh," I say, and begin walking toward the house.

"Molly," he calls after me. I turn. "Be careful. Bobby Matthews is a grifter. And he doesn't care about anyone but himself."

19

Fred's drinking coffee and writing on a thick pad attached to a clip board. An open medical encyclopedia and several other books litter the table.

"Waiting for me?" I say, helping myself to a cup of coffee and sitting down at the table.

"Hey, cousin," Fred says. He stacks up the books and papers carefully and lays his pen diagonally across the top. "I, uh, feel a certain responsibility here. You know, to protect my family."

I lean into the table, put my cup down, and hold on to it with both hands. I know what's coming. All these years of waiting for someone to grab the hook and drag the whole sordid mess to the surface. I'm sorry it's Fred, though. Fred who lost his own father the year before I lost Cliff. Who suffered Gran's annual get togethers and all the other torments of being a member of the Evers clan. Partners in misery, Fred and me. And that whole thing with the dog and Uncle Ed. Why did it have to be Fred? Better to have a stranger, someone who didn't know you. Like Officer Campion. No, not him. . .

"Molly?" Fred is calling. "You okay, Molly?"

"Huh?"

"Geeze, cousin. Don't scare me like that. You like, zoned out. I thought you were having a seizure or something. You sure you're all right?"

"Yeah, I'm okay. Sorry." I take a quick gulp of coffee and hold the cup up to hide my quivering chin.

"What's that?" Fred asks pointing at my coffee.

"What?" I put the cup on the table and turn it around.

"That," Fred says, taking my hand and pulling the hidden tags from my sleeve. I shrug and let him pull apart the plastic cord and lay the tags on the table.

"Thanks," I tell him. "I've been hiding those all night. What's going on?"

"Well, like I was saying, the state lab boys are working on the evidence."

I pick up the cup again and nod over the ellipse.

"Nothing conclusive yet, you know. These things take time. Lord knows even new evidence is hard to decipher, but stuff that's been buried for years, well. It's gonna be a while before they can put the pieces together and prove anything. If they can ever prove anything."

I nod again, and shiver as the goose bumps crawl up the back of my neck.

"If it was anybody else, I mean. Molly you're family, and I'm worried about you."

"I know." I drink the rest of my coffee in short gulps.

"I mean it's his wife, his car, his temper. Bobbie is the obvious suspect."

"Bobbie?"

"That's why I don't understand you going out with him. Bobbie Matthews, for Christ-sake."

"How did you know that Bobby Matthews was my date?"

"Howard Santini. He said he saw the two of you at the "Trout."

"I see."

"Now, don't get mad, cousin. Howard was surprised, is all. And he didn't actually mean to tell me, you know. It just sort of slipped out."

"That's okay." I tell him, placing my empty cup on the table and leaning forward. "I didn't actually know it was Bobby Matthews until tonight."

"You didn't know?"

"Well, after you left me at the hospital the other day, I was finishing up my lunch when this man came in. We were the only two people in the cafeteria and, well, I guess I kinda picked him up."

"You picked him up? " Fred says under his breath. "Classic."

"Well, he was choking, well, at least I thought he was. But when I got there he was okay. And then we talked. He said his name was Rob, and he invited me out. He seemed like a nice guy,

"Oh."

"He just seems so nice. Do you really think he killed his wife?"

"I don't know what to think," Fred says. He gets up and pours himself some coffee. With his back still to me, he says, "Bobby and I go way back. Charlie Bauer and me and Bobby. Since the sixth grade." He turns, still holding the coffee carafe.

"Charlie Bauer, the Mayor?" I ask, holding up my cup for a refill. He pours the last of the coffee into my cup and sets the carafe in the sink.

"How do you know about Charlie?"

"Something Bobby said about Charlie and a palm tree and a keg of beer."

"The island," Fred says, smiling. The he sits back down and reaches across the table to take my hand. "Seriously though, I mean this. Be careful with Bobby. If he did it, and he finds out we've found Charlene, he could be dangerous."

"He knows," I say.

"What? How?" Fred lets go of my hand.

"Well, I told him. I'm sorry, it just slipped out in conversation."

"Shit, Mollly. What did he say?"

"Well." I close my eyes and try to remember. "He looked shocked. Then he said that they were happy, but that after she had the baby she got depressed and started drinking. He said she made up stories and left him a couple of times, but that she always came back. He said he loved her." I open my eyes.

"Is that it?"

"Well, later he said something about starting over. Rewinding the past, or something like that."

"Molly, this is not good. Bobby Matthews is a suspect in the murder of his wife. And the murder of the other person in the car too. Promise me you're not going to go out with him again."

"I don't know, Fred. Do you really think he did it? I mean, do you really think he did?"

"Yeah," Fred says. "I think my old friend Bobby Matthews killed his wife. Maybe he didn't mean to do it but, I think he murdered her, and he put her in the car and pushed the car out to the thin part of the frozen lake and watched it go under. That's what I think, but I can't prove it. Yet. I think you'll be a lot safer if you steer clear of him."

"Oh my god," I say, almost dropping my cup. The thick weave of my cardigan can't keep away the chill I feel.

"What's the matter?" Fred leans in and steadies my hand.

"He was talking about Charlie Bauer and the palm tree, and the diving float. He said that he thought that's where he got the idea."

"What idea?"

"He said how the barrels rusted and the float flipped over. How they opened up the rest of the barrels and . . . and let it sink to the bottom."

20

I am still cold in the morning. The snug quilt and quickly rising temperatures seem only to take the edge off the chill in my body. I abandon the quilt and dress quickly in jeans and a T shirt . I consider throwing on the jacket. but decide it will warm up, so why bother. I hurry down to the kitchen where the smell of fresh coffee welcomes me.

The kitchen is oddly quiet for a house with young children, but the coffee pot is full and I hurry to the counter to pour myself some. The warmth of the cup in my hands helps chase away my chill and I lift it to my lips just to inhale the steamy aroma.

Through the kitchen window I see a group of people splashing and laughing around the Evers dock. I lower my cup, lean over the sink and use the palm of my hand to wipe away the steamy condensation from the glass. Fred and Carol and the girls are pushing the pontoon boat into deeper water. Suddenly Fred scoops up an armful of water and throws it in Carol's direction. She sidesteps the bulk of the splash and slaps the water, hard, sending a wide arc of cascading water at Fred. The girls and the dog join in and eventually they are all soaked and laughing. Fred barks an order and they return to the work of freeing the pontoon from its sandy mooring.

I absentmindedly lift my cup and swallow a gulp of hot coffee. It burns down my throat and brings the tears that I was trying to hold back, streaming down my face. My hand on the burning spot in my chest, I cough and inhale deeply as I drop my cup down on the counter.

"You okay?"

I turn, hand still clutching my chest and tears still streaming, to see Billy Campion sitting at the table with a bowl of cereal. "Hot coffee," I manage to say.

"Coffee's not good for you," he says seriously.

"Probably not," I agree and sit down across from him with my cup. "What are you doing all alone in here? It looks like the action is all out there."

"You're here," he says, scooping the last Cheerio from the bowl with his finger and popping it in his mouth.

He's got a point. Come on Molly, a kindergartner could handle this better. I imagine basketball bugs as Billy draws up his knees and balances his heels on the chair seat. Don't poke, I remind myself. "Okay," I say.

"They're going to take the pontoon out," he volunteers. "I don't want to go."

"Oh. You know, I used to come here, to Crooked Lake when I was a kid." I sip my coffee and look out through the screen door at the lake. "The last time I was here, I was about your age. Fred and I used to walk around the lake and catch minnows and frogs. Nobody had pontoons then, they had rowboats and fishing boats with small motors."

"And they walked five miles to school everyday, up hill, in three feet of snow."

I look up and he is smiling. "Oh, you've heard this one before," I say. I've made a connection. Don't blow it Molly. I try to remember something from an article I read to help me dig deeper. Don't ask questions, let him do the talking.

He raises his eyebrows and rolls his eyes. "Dad wants me to appreciate history."

"Your dad worries about you," I say.

"I know."

"He told me you lost your mother." Shut up Molly. You're going too fast. I sip my coffee and hope I haven't ended the conversation.

"Didn't lose her," he says, dropping his chin into the space between his knees and staring hard at his empty cereal bowl. "She died."

"That's what I meant. I'm sorry."

"It was a long time ago."

"I lost . . . I mean, my father died too, when I was eleven." Why am I telling him this? "It was awful. I wanted the world to stop turning but it wouldn't. I still miss him. Do you miss your mom."

"Not really."

I can't help it. I look up, my eyes wide and my stomach suddenly knotted. He isn't looking at me, he's looking at the wood grain of the table, like it was a crystal ball and he was searching for something lost. I can feel heat in my cheeks and a tickle under my eyes. I reach up to brush away any escaping tears.

"I don't remember her. Except her laugh. I remember she laughed a lot, and she sang." He looks up suddenly and catches me rubbing my eyes. "I heard her sing when Kyle got hurt, you know. She was there. She was like . . . an angel or something. Is Kyle going to die too?"

"I don't know."

"Kyle's mean and kinda stuck up, but he's the only one I can talk to. He's the only one that understands. If Kyle dies, I won't have anybody."

"What about Charlene and Frieda. Couldn't they be your friends?"

He looks at me like I suggested he eat worms.

"You know, you can talk to me if you want." I let the idea hang in the air between us and sip my coffee.

"Charlie and Freddy are okay, for girls. But I'm not like them." he says. "Every year when we make things in school for Mother's Day, they have someone to give it to. They have someone who packs their lunches, calls them by special nicknames, makes them cakes for their birthdays, gives them an extra money for treats when they go to the movies, hugs them - for no reason at all."

"What about Yvonne? Doesn't she do some of those things?"

"No. Except the store-bought cake she got me once, but it was chocolate. I hate chocolate cake. I hate Yvonne, too."

"But your dad likes her."

"No, he doesn't."

"He doesn't?"

"Nope."

"Why does he go out with her, if he doesn't like her."

"She asks him, but she's safe. They can go out, but he won't fall in love with her or anything."

"Why?"

"He just won't."

"Because he still loves your mother?"

"No, I mean he does still love her, but it's not that."

"What do you think it is?"

"She's not right. She doesn't make him tingle."

"Tingle?" This is not a term I'd associate with Deputy Sheriff Will Campion.

"You know, like a spark, like fireworks. My dad says that when people love each other it's like a spark gets lit. There's no spark with Yvonne. She's a dud."

Out of the mouths of babes, I think, sipping coffee to cover up my smile. But the mention of fireworks reminds me of that summer twenty years ago, when I was no older than Billy, and I sabotaged Uncle Ed's boat. The fireworks that we all watched from the shore that night were the final moments of Uncle Ed's life, and it was my fault. Rewinding the past, wasn't that what Bobby Matthews said? If only I could.

21

When Fred and Carol and the girls return from their wrestling match with the pontoon, they are muddy and wet. Carol pilots the girls to the bathroom for showers while Fred hoses down the dog in the yard. I'm refilling my coffee cup when he gives up chasing the dog, pulls a towel off the clothesline and splashes into the house.

"Hey, cousin," he says, smiling, while he heels off his shoes near the door. "Missed a good water fight," he tells Billy. Billy shrugs and takes his bowl and spoon to the sink behind me. Fred shakes like a dog, flinging water in a halo around his head, and folds the towel across his shoulders. "We're taking the old barge out for a spin, got room for two more."

"Thanks, but I have paperwork to do."

"What about you, Billy? You comin' with us? Can't let Charlene and Frieda have all the fun." Billy shakes his head and turns on the faucet to rinse his dishes. I feel him shaking behind me.

"Kind of reminds me of you, cousin," Fred says, pulling on the towel ends and looking up at the ceiling. "What was it you used to say? If a person stands still in the same place long enough, people will eventually forget you're there?"

"Pot calling the kettle black if you ask me," Carol calls from the stairway. "We're nearly ready and you're still standin there like a statue, dripping on the floor."

"Duty calls," Fred says, saluting Carol as he passes her on the steps, and dropping the wet towel on her.

"Man's just a small child himself," she says as he double steps up the stairs. "Billy, honey, you sure you won't come with us?"

"No, thank you, Mrs. Evers," he says, slipping between us and out the door.

"Sure wish I could get him interested in something," Carol says. "Is it okay with you if he stays here? I mean, you haven't got a date or anything." She frowns at me as she uses the towel to soak up Fred's drips by the door.

"No. I don't have a date."

"I thought maybe your date last night, I mean, you were talking in your sleep."

"I was?"

"Well, singing, actually."

"Singing?"

"Yeah, Molly, really, Bobby Matthews of all people."

"Carol, I didn't know it was Bobby Matthews. Really. I didn't know."

Carol stands up with the wet towel in her hands. "That's what Fred said. God Molly, Bobby of all people."

"I'm not going out with him again."

"No?"

"No."

"I'm glad. Are you sure you don't want to come with us? Fred hardly ever takes time off, especially week days. He's working something out. He always does this. He goes fishing or takes the girls to the water park. Gets his mind off whatever it is he's working on, and that's when he figures it out."

The girls run through the room and out the door. They stop on the porch and talk to Billy, who is sitting in the wicker chair.

When Fred comes down and they leave, Carol turns to call through the screen door, "There's some chicken salad in the fridge. And some fresh sun tea."

Fred's dog has pestered Billy into tossing a frisbee. Not a giant step, but at least the boy is interacting with someone. I spread my paperwork out on the kitchen table and check off the steps the clerk outlined as I complete them. Uncle Ed's death certificate lists the cause of death as "accidental drowning, with contributing factors." In parentheses under that it reads "post traumatic stress disorder, alcohol and prescription medication."

Yeah, right. Doesn't say "sabotage by eleven-year-old niece." Tears blur the paper and I open my eyes wide, breathe in hard, and try to blink the tears away. Ed Evers was just thirty-one when he died. My age.

"You okay?"

I clear my throat and rub the wet off my cheek with the side of my hand before I turn. "I'm fine," I tell Billy.

"My dad says it's okay to cry." He stands with his back to the door but his hand still holding the door handle.

"Yeah?" I say, motioning him to join me. He lets go of the door, walks a few steps while running his hand across the countertop. He stops behind the chair next to me and holds the chair back with both hands.

"He says it lets the bad stuff out." Now he's rocking slightly and biting his lower lip.

"Billy?"

"Kyle never cries,." he says, as tears squeeze from the corners of his eyes. "Never."

"Billy," I say, leaning over to guide him into the chair. "Your dad is right. It's okay to cry. In fact, I think it's necessary."

He sits heavily and lowers his head. I stack my papers into a small pile while I compose my thoughts. "Kyle's your best friend?" I ask Billy.

"Yeah. Sort of."

"Tell me about him."

"He's like me. We're both eleven. His birthday's first, though, so he's older. Just three days Kyle makes a big deal about it, like it's a contest or something. You know?"

"Kyle likes to win?"

"Well, not win exactly. I think what he really likes, you know, is to see someone else lose. Me, usually. I'm taller than he is too. We were even last summer but I grew a lot this year, and that made him mad too. That's why he got the bike. A mountain bike. Twenty-one speeds. He couldn't beat me on his old bike, so he got a new one. Kyle always gets anything he wants. I still would have beat him, though. If he hadn't cheated."

"He cheated?"

"Yeah. Kicked my tire. Knocked me into the weeds. Messed up my bike real good. Called me a . . . loser."

"You're not a loser, Billy." I put my hand across his clenched fist on the table. "I'll bet if Kyle could talk to you right now, he'd tell you that. He's probably really sorry for what he said."

Billy's quiet for a moment, then whispers, "Mackinac Island Fudge."

"Mackinac Island Fudge?"

"Yeah." The tears are falling freely down his cheeks, now. He pulls his hand from mine and leans into the back of the chair. "We always race to the swimming hole," he says." First one in the water wins and the loser buys ice cream, after." He sniffs loudly and wipes his nose and cheeks with the back of his hand. "Mackinac Island Fudge is Kyle's favorite. He yelled it . . . when he swung out on the rope." His chin quivers. "He cheated, you know, so I told him to 'drop dead'."

22

"Do you think he'll die?" Billy asks, as he pours sun tea into a large tumbler.

I look up from the sandwiches I'm making and say, "I don't know, Billy. I don't know."

"Well," says Billy. "If he does, it'll be something else he beats me at. I guess that'd make him happy. Bein' first always makes Kyle happy."

I can't think of anything to say. I place the sandwiches on plates and take them to the table. We sit across from each other and eat the chicken salad Carol left for us. Billy picks pieces of crust from his sandwich and nibbles them.

"Are you really Mr. Evers' cousin? Charlie says you are."

"It's true," I say. "Fred is my first cousin. My only first cousin, as a matter of fact."

"I don't have any cousins. Hey, was your dad the one that was killed in the fireworks?"

"What?"

"My dad says one of Mr. Evers' uncles was killed in an accident, with fireworks. He won't let me do bottle rockets, you know. Says it's too dangerous."

"Well, your dad's right. Bottle rockets are dangerous. And no. Ed Evers was my mother's brother. My dad was Cliff Swain.

"Your last name is Swain?"

"Yep."

Billy smiles broadly and says, "You're Molly Swain."

"Yes," I say, puzzled by his sudden brightening.

"I have something that belongs to you, Molly Swain. It's at my house. Can we go? I can't believe it. You're Molly Swain."

"Something of mine?"

He takes a big bite of his sandwich and nods his head. It takes him only minutes to finish the whole sandwich and drink a full tumbler of iced tea.

"Come on, Molly Swain," he says while he puts his dishes in the sink. "Come on."

"Okay," I tell him. "But first we need to clean up our dishes, and then we need to write a note for Carol, so she won't worry.

"Okay, okay," he says, turning to fill the sink with water and soap. "You write the note."

He washes and rinses his plate and tumbler and sets them in the drying rack. I point to the bowl and spoon on the counter. He washes them too and turns to watch me eat the last bite of my sandwich. He takes my empty plate and watches while I drink my tea. Whatever he thinks he's found, it's blocked out the accident for a little while. If only to keep his mind off Kyle Matthews, I'll indulge him. His father's been doing repairs on lake properties for years, I expect his father let him play at the work sites, but can't imagine what could have possibly survived twenty years in a rental cottage.

"You know, Billy. I have to stop by the Clerk's office in Chandler and drop off this paperwork first." I take the last sip of tea and hold out the tumbler. "And I don't know where you live."

"We live in Cascade," he says, taking the tumbler and quickly brushing the wash rag around the inside. Then he rinses and places it with the other clean dishes. "It's not far, really. It'll only take a minute."

I write a short note to Carol and Fred and we're on our way.

Billy Campion paces in the hallway outside the Clerk's office while she checks my documents, rechecks them, asks for my ID. She's copying my license number when the phone rings.

"I really have to take this," she apologizes.

I look back at Billy, standing with his hands half in his pockets, his thumbs hooked into his belt loops like a blue jeans commercial. I shrug and nod my head toward the clerk on the telephone. Billy unhooks one thumb, takes off his cap one-handed and scratches behind his ear. Then he replaces the ball cap, pulling the bill down hard, and re-hooks his thumb in the belt loop. Standing there, with his face half hidden by the cap, he could easily be mistaken for his father.

When we finally reach the Campion house, Billy excitedly tells me to stop. The house is a squat craftsman bungalow, squeezed between two victorian style cottages. Set back from the street, with no driveway, its minimalist porch is almost even with the backside of the gingerbread adorned wraparound verandahs of its neighbors. We park in the street. Billy runs up the cement walk ahead of me and holds open the door. The smell of varnish and lemons draws me into the house. Billy rushes up the staircase, leaving me in the entryway, which is really just a hallway down the center of the house. I can see down the hall and out through the kitchen door where a rusted swing set and an alleyway take up most of the Campion back yard. I step further in, listening to the sounds of rummaging overhead. The living room is small, with wide, dark trim. A green tile fireplace flanked by built-in bookcases takes up the end wall. Small rectangular windows of stained glass, above the bookcases, throw shards of colored light on the furniture and floor. I have to give Will Campion credit. This is an exquisite, yet comfortable room. I walk to the fireplace and pivot, taking in the room's warm simplicity. Photographs are displayed on the bookcase. An antique wedding picture. The kind where the bride stands and the groom is seated. Beside it, a woman's portrait in a shell-encrusted frame and a candid photo in a plain frame of a different, very pregnant, woman. Behind the woman I recognize Campion's stained glass window and bookcase. This must be Will Campion's wife. Billy's mother. I feel suddenly ashamed, like I'm poking through someone else's underwear drawer. Billy's footsteps pound down the stairs and I quickly turn and pretend to be admiring the fireplace.

"Here it is," he beams. "It's yours, isn't it?"

The air leaves the room. My heart shoves ice water through my veins, squeezing my head in a liquid vice, making my fingertips go numb. I lean into the fireplace mantel and close my eyes. "Breathe, Molly," my chilled brain screams;"Breathe!"

Billy barely notices my frozen expression, or the color drained from my face. He stands triumphantly, his arms extended, the fancy candy tin, my candy tin, the one I buried when I was eleven, balanced on his upturned palms.

"See," Billy says, pulling the box into his body, prying the two halves apart as he crosses the room.

I stand transfixed, unable to look away as the box yawns open. A rush of breath escapes as I wait for the evidence of my crime to spill out. The box is open. Nothing falls out. No screwdriver, no oarlocks, no library book, nothing. I step forward, try to get a better look.

"This is you, isn't it. Isn't it?" He pulls a sliver of yellow plastic from the box and holds it up for me to see. "Molly Swain, Grade 6," written in the large round letters I preferred in my youth, on a yellow paper encased in plastic. Old water stains obscure the otter logo and the school crest.

"My library card," I sigh.

"There was more," Billy says, giving me the card before sitting down with the two halves of the box in his hands."My dad kept the screw diver, but the rest was all rusted and moldy so he made me throw it away. I cleaned up the box real good. I thought you'd be my age. I mean, it says grade six."

"Yeah. Well, I was your age - eleven, the last summer I came to Crooked Lake." Until now, that is.

"How come?"

I manage to sit down next to Billy on the couch. I rub the corroded edge of the plastic with my thumb. I wondered what had happened to this card. I blamed Helen for losing it in the packing that summer. It had expired of course, and I got a new one. But this one was special, Cliff, who encouraged my appetite for books, had encased it in plastic so I wouldn't wear it out.

"How come you quit coming to Crooked Lake?" Billy asks again.

"My Uncle Ed," I tell him. My adam's apple feels more like a grapefruit lodged in my throat. I can almost smell cordite as I look at the pieces of tin in Billy's hands. "When I was eleven, my Uncle Ed . . . the one your dad told you about . . . well, you know. He died in a boat accident out on the lake. I did something, and then Uncle Ed died, and I couldn't take it back."

"Like me an' Kyle," Billy says, closing the box.

My strangled sob joins his and we sit together on the couch in the Campion living room, my arm across his shoulder, his face buried in his hands. Billy's anguish is quiet, deep. I can feel the sharp shudders as he lets go of the tears he's been holding for his mother and the guilt he's been harboring about Kyle. My own tears are a surprise. They roll unabated down my face, pulling on a barbed hook in my throat. I am crying for Cliff, and for Gran, and for the boy Uncle Ed was before he went to war, the boy in the photograph in Gran's cottage. And I am crying for myself, for all of the time wasted in anger and fear. I cry until there are no more tears. Until the "bad stuff" is out.

And then we sit for a minute, as quiet as the stains of colored light on the carpet, alone in our separate tragedies. I think about Cliff as I stare at the rectangle of yellow in my hand. Of all of the things I lost that summer, the library card was the last thing I thought I'd ever find. The evidence I was sure would be found, the evidence that tied me to my uncle's murder, no longer exists. Why doesn't that make me feel better?

"You can have it," Billy says, his voice husky from crying. He pushes the tin box into my hand.

23

We stop at the Shoreline Diner, before returning to Fred's. The familiar sound of the bell above the door announces our entry, and Flo nods as we pass the counter. From our booth next to the window, we can see the occasional car pass by on Crooked Lake Road, and hear the crunch of gravel when a dusty blue mini van turns into the Shoreline parking lot.

"What'll it be?" Flo asks.

"Vanilla ice cream on a peanut butter cookie," Billy says, turning away from the window. "With butterscotch syrup, please."

"Just a scoop of vanilla for me." I smile, and then add, "Can I get sprinkles?"

"Just for you," Flo answers. She calls out the order as she walks behind the counter. "A single vanilla with sprinkles, and a Campion Special."

"I gotta go to the bathroom," Billy says, sliding across the bench and heading into the back hall. He is just out of sight when the bell above the door jingles and Yvonne Potter steps into the diner. She sits at the counter and orders coffee, "to go."

"Got some of them fudge cookies you like," Flo tells her. "Fresh out the oven."

"Just coffee," Yvonne answers, counting change out on the countertop and making sure the lid is securely on the coffee before picking it up. She doesn't see me until she turns to leave. "Miss Swain? Where have you been?"

I shrug and smile as she balances the coffee and walks toward me. "I have been trying to reach you all day. I've left several messages on your cell phone."

"Really?" I tell her while pulling my phone from my purse. I flip it open and nothing lights up. "The battery must be dead, Im sorry. What can I do for you?"

"Well, um . ." Suddenly Yvonne seems to be wordless. She looks all around the empty diner then breathes a heavy sigh as she sits down. She taps the sides of the paper coffee cup with her nails. "I need to talk to you. I um . . . can you meet me at your mother's cottage, say, in an hour?"

"The cottage? Sure, I guess I could. What's up?"

Flo puts the ice creams between us on the table. Yvonne looks at them for a moment, bites her lower lip, then says, "I have to go. You'll meet me?"

"Sure," I tell her. "In an hour."

After Yvonne leaves, Billy comes out from the shadows of the back hall. "What did she want?" he asks.

"Just some real estate business," I tell him.

We eat our ice cream in silence. The afternoon has worn us both out. Billy eats slowly, staring at the table between us. He frowns, as if trying to align the scattered boomerangs in the formica into neat rows. The excitement of the afternoon has withdrawn and left behind a brooding child, lost in the pain of growing up. To be honest, I feel a little lost myself. All these years, trying to push everything "Crooked Lake" away. Brooding. Blaming that summer when I was eleven for all my inadequacies, all my failures. My ice cream, even with sprinkles, suddenly tastes sour. I leave it half eaten and watch Billy lick butterscotch sauce from his fingers.

"That boy is unnaturally quiet," Flo says as I hand her a twenty. "Reminds me a lot of you at that age."

"I can't believe you remember me at all," I tell her, feeling the edge of the library card sticking out of my wallet.

"Oh heavens, yes. I remember you and the professor comin' in here. He was a real good tipper, you know. And I knew your whole family, of course. Ed mostly, he was in my class in high school. Enlisted with my brother James right after graduation. And little Helen. How is your mom? I sort of expected her to come back here, after your Gran died."

"Helen's fine. She's got her charities and she keeps busy. "Did you know my father? Not Cliff, I mean my biological father."

Flo hesitates, the register drawer open and her hand across the bills inside. She looks at me briefly, before pushing the twenty into a slot. "Well," she says slowly, looking down as if talking to the money in the drawer. "I reckon I know him. It's a small town and I know prit-near everybody. But, you see, Helen was a lot younger than me. And she never told anybody. Not even after you were born. So yeah, I probably know him, but I don't know who he is, if you get my drift."

"Oh," I say, letting that thought soak into my head while I watch her pull smaller bills from the drawer. The tiny enameled sandal charms on her bracelet remind me of the night twenty years ago. "You said, that night. The night that we were here and you found shoes for me, the night Ed died. You said that night changed your life."

"Oh, my, yes. It sure did," she says, smiling. "We were all standin' out in the parking lot, watchin' the fireworks like everybody else. Of course then we didn't know it was Ed, and that he wouldn't be , well, you know. It was so glorious, though, all them bursts of light, and I just... well, I don't know what got into me, but I turned and gave ol' Harley a great big kiss. Right on the mouth. Right there in the parking lot, with customers and everything. He was so surprised he practically fainted. I figured he'd fire me for sure. Harley bein' such a private person and all. But later that night, when we were closing up, he says, 'Flossie - marry me.' Just like that. And I did."

"I thought you dated Uncle Ed."

"Oh sure, I dated Ed Evers in high school. Even wrote to him when him and James were in Viet Nam. But Ed changed, you know. Stopped writing, even to his momma. He took James' dying real hard, you know. He told me once, it should'a been him. Like it was his fault, when it was nobody's fault, really. Imagine feeling like that."

"Yeah, imagine," I say taking my change.

24

I'm still thinking about my conversation with Flo at the diner as I walk between the cottages toward the lake. Uncle Ed blamed himself for Flo's brother's death - but Flo didn't? "Nobody's fault," she said. "Nobody's fault. Things happen." She could have been talking about Billy Campion and his friend Kyle. Or she could have been talking about me. But I wasn't just there, and it didn't just happen. I did something, I made something happen.

I'm late. Weather reports were predicting a storm coming and I didn't want to leave Billy home alone. Fred and Carol didn't return till nearly six thirty. By then Fred's neighbor had blocked the drive with a motor home so I left my car and walked down Crooked Lake Road and took the shortcut through the land bridge around the lake.

I don't see Yvonne's mini-van, and I can't call her because I left my cell phone charging in the car. It must be nearly seven now and I'm wishing I'd brought my jacket. Even though it isn't dark yet, the back side of the cottage is nearly lost in chilly shadows. Sunlight, orange where it touches the treetops across the lake, streams golden through the cottage, lighting up the porch door glass and the kitchen windows that Campion replaced. Even the older panes in the window have been washed and they channel the light entering through the lakeside windows into sharp yellow rectangles on the ground. So, Will Campion is the kind of man who fixes things and cleans up the mess. What does that mean?

The sound of a motor in the water draws me to the lake side of the cottage. A large pontoon boat, just off shore, is gently rocking against the dock.

"Hello," I call out. "Yvonne, is that you?"

A male figure rises from one of the cushioned benches on the boat. Silhouetted against the setting sun, I don't recognize him until he speaks.

"Sorry to disappoint," Bobby Matthews says, walking toward me on the dock. "Nobody here but me."

"What are you doing here?"

He looks startled, then smiles. "Oh, you mean, what am I doing tied to your dock?"

I nod.

"I'm looking at the future, Molly. See this row of cottages. Run down rentals, all of them. Revenue negative eyesores."

I look back at the empty cabins, cabins I loathed once, often wished would be struck by lightning and burn to the ground, and remember the laughter of children playing in the water, their parents cooking hot dogs and burgers on grills by the docks. For a moment I have a clear recollection of Howard Santini, a skinny dark haired boy with a gaggle of brothers and sisters playing with beach balls in the water a few cottages down. "It's not so bad," I hear myself say.

"Oh, Molly, Molly," Bobby says. "That's sentiment talking. Not reality. Let me show you."

"I'm meeting someone," I say turning from the dock, hoping Yvonne will materialize from the shadows.

"It will just take a minute, Molly." I feel his hand on my arm. "I'm sure your date will wait. I would."

I'm only slightly charmed by his smile. Fred's warning still rings in my head. But looking at him, smiling, I'm sure Fred must be wrong. I'm torn between imagining what he might be capable of and the memory of the pasta bajoul and his hand

139

holding mine. And what am I going to do, anyway?Go running down the shoreline, making a fool of myself? "Maybe, just for a moment," I say, and let him guide me aboard the pontoon where he adjusts the cushion on a narrow bench and invites me to sit down.

"My development is going to replace this slum with spacious, Club Med kinds of cabins," he says. He pulls up the mooring line and pushes off the dock with his foot. My heart thumps in my throat as I watch the shoreline recede and feel the boat rock on the waves. It's like I'm eleven again and Uncle Ed is about to throw me overboard. I grip the boat railing and think about jumping. Bobby balances himself behind the wheel, revs the engine and maneuvers the pontoon in reverse until we are about 50 feet from the shore. I breathe deeply, trying to control my racing heart, while he locks the wheel and stands next to me. "Just imagine it, Molly. Year round rentals, swimming and boating in the summer, snowmobiles and ice fishing in the winter. I'm thinking, you know, a clubhouse with upscale restaurants. A casino atmosphere with big name entertainers and one of those exclusive spas. It'll be glorious, don't you think?"

"Glorious," I say, looking back at the shoreline and feeling the boat motor vibrate through my seat cushion. The sun is dropping behind the trees and I can barely see the outline of the cottage against the pines. A tiny sliver of moon hangs in the pale blue just above the roof peak. I squint, trying to make out the shoreline and suddenly two bright lights sweep through the cottage and spill out the windows onto the dock. Just as suddenly they go out. I hold the urge to scream across the water, "Yvonne, I'm out here!" The boat's vibration changes and I turn to see Bobby standing at the wheel.

"Of course we're going to have to excavate a lot of sand," he says, changing gears and leaning into the steering wheel. "There's a kind of shelf on this beach that makes it too shallow for the bigger boats." The pontoon churns through the water while I white-knuckle the railing and balance awkwardly on the bench. I'm remembering that drop off. The place where the sand ledge suddenly falls off and angles steeply into the deep waters of the lake. The place where I stood all those years ago, waiting to be noticed, to be missed I kind of envy people like Robert Matthews who simply change the landscape or reconfigure nature when it suits them. People like me run away, never get past the drop off. Never take a chance in the deeper water, or the family chaos on the shore. That's me, always somewhere in the middle, the shallows, with my toes in the sand and my head just above water. I can almost taste the lake.

"I want to go back." I tell him.

"Sure, sure. In a minute. I want to show you something."

We are almost in the center of the lake when he cuts the engine. The few lights that dot the shoreline seem incredibly far away. Night is descending and it's very quiet. The kind of quiet I used to like. Just the lapping of the waves against the pontoons, and small murmurs of the boat as it settles itself in the water. I feel goose bumps from the cool lake breeze and then Bobby's hand on my shoulder.

"Isn't this something?" he says. For awhile we just drift. His light touch on my shoulder, my firm grip on the railing. I force myself to relax, try to imagine the water's surface is a vast green lawn. "I can walk to the edge," I tell myself and look wistfully at the shore.

"This used to be my favorite spot," Bobby says. "You can damn near see everything from here. On a clear night you can almost hear God breathe, you know? Hey, I got some beer in the cooler, Molly, want one?" I shake my head, no. He opens the cooler and takes out two cans.

"Char and I used to come here all the time," he says, opening both cans and taking a sip from one. "Yeah, those were the days. We'd come out here, have a few beers, take off our clothes and jump in. Hey, Molly, want to go skinny-dipping?"

I struggle to breathe normally. There is water all around me. Twenty years and I'm still terrified of the lake. "I don't swim," I tell him.

"Really? Wow, Molly. That's a shame." He drinks the entire can and pitches the empty across the water. "Nothing like swimming under the stars. You ever look at them? The stars. I mean really look. That's Cassiopeia over there and the dippers up there. And that bright little cluster right there, just above my development - that's Aquarius. That's what I'm going to name the resort. Aquarius." He takes a long sip from the second can.

I look up and try to remember the constellations. The darkening sky makes it easier to pick out the stars and I'm pretty sure he's got them wrong. I don't know about Cassiopeia but I'm pretty sure the dippers are due north? Something Cliff once told me about the 19th century American slaves making their way north by following the dipper.

A series of chirps echo over the water. I watch Bobby unclip a cell phone from his belt and flip it open. "Update on the boy," he says. "I have to take this." He cups the phone to his ear and moves toward the opposite side of the deck. "Yes, this is Robert Matthews. Yes, I'll hold." He shrugs, turns his back and leans on the railing.

I look back at the sky. Clouds are rushing in to obscure the stars, but I'm pretty sure I can find the big dipper. I stand, steady myself with a knee into the bench cushion, and search the the cluster of stars over the cottage. Aquarius? Maybe. I try to make out the familiar outline of the cottage through the gathering dark. According to Will Campion it's probably the last of the original cottages that, how did he put it? "haven't been "renovated to death." Well, if Bobby Matthews has his way, it won't be renovated, it'll be bulldozed. That makes me a little sad. Behind me Bobby clears his throat.

"Hello, Dr. Mills. Yes, has he come to? What? He what? Yes. . . Yes. I do understand. But I thought you said . . . no. No. Thank you. You've done enough!"

I turn to see Bobby lean out over the rail and vomit. A growling, horrible animal sound follows and I watch as his back stiffens and he hurls the cell phone out over the water. I hear the sploosh as it hits and then Bobby screams into the darkness. "Bitch!" He screams again, louder. "Bitch! All these years and you're still screwing with me! Don't think I don't know it was you! Of course it was you. You couldn't just let it be, could you? You just couldn't stay away, could you? Damn you, Charlene! I should have pushed that damn Mustang over a cliff and let you burn to hell. It was all coming together, for me, Char. I'm a success now, people respect me. But you just couldn't let me be happy, could you? Could you? But why the boy, Char. Our boy. You just had to hurt me, didn't you. Take away my boy, you knew that would hurt me, didn't you? You just had to take him." Bobby stands at the railing, his shoulders sagging, his head down, sobbing. A gut wrenching, horrible sob. And then, suddenly he stands straight and turns to look at me.

"I guess you heard," he says, matter of factly.

"I'm sorry," I say softly, "about your son."

"Don't play with me," he snarls. "I know you heard. Yeah, I did it. I killed her, my wife. Strangled her, if you want to know."

"Don't want to know," I say, closing my eyes and wishing I were someplace else. Anyplace else.

"Doesn't matter now," he says. "She made me do it, you know. She just wouldn't stop nagging me. That night, she said she'd had enough, she was leaving me, taking the boy. Oh, I'd been drinking, sure, but she just wouldn't listen to me. I didn't care if she left, really. She was a stupid woman. But I couldn't let her take my boy, could I? She went too far. She asked for it, deserved what she got. I feel bad about the Chavez kid though. Wrong time, wrong place. He came back for a shovel his old man left and saw her. Couldn't let him go, could I?"

"I guess not."

"Brings up an interesting point, doesn't it?"

"It does?"

"What do I do with Molly Evers?"

"Molly Swain," I correct him.

"Molly Swain," he repeats. "I like you Molly, I really do. But you can see the problem, can't you? Funny how these things happen, isn't it? Char and the gardener's kid, and now you and Campion's boy." He takes a step toward me.

"What about Billy?" I ask, my back pressing into the guard rail.

"Well, he's responsible, isn't he? Damn kid was always getting my boy in trouble. Should have been him that died, not my Kyle."

"It's not his fault," I tell him. "Billy's just a kid. I won't let you hurt him."

"You won't? Oh, Molly. Molly. You don't have a choice, do you? No one knows you're out here, do they?" He crosses the deck before I understand his intent. A sudden horrible image flashes across my mind. Uncle Ed cleaning his gun after shooting the dog.

"I'm sorry," he says reaching for my wrist and wrenching my hand from the railing. "I really am. You're going to have an accident, Molly. It's too bad you don't swim." I twist and try to hit him. He only grasps my wrists tighter.

"No, don't..." I say, pulling away. I try to kick him, but only succeed in losing what traction I had on the decking.

"I'm sorry," he says again, holding my wrists firmly, forcing my own knuckles into my throat, tilting me further over the railing.

"No!" I manage to scream as my own weight finishes the job and I tumble into the water.

"Please!" I try to yell, coughing up water when I surface, trying hard to kick as water fills my shoes.

"Don't fight it, Molly," he tells me, leaning over the rail and cupping a hand to his mouth. "Close your eyes and just let yourself sink. I've thought about doing it myself; it isn't so bad. Just close your eyes and let go. All your troubles will be over."

The shoes are full now, and pulling me down. I catch a breath and go under struggling with the ties and then pulling them off. When I surface and gasp for air, Bobby is already starting the engine and putting the pontoon in gear. I tread water and watch it recede into the darkness. Above me, in a patch of clear sky a sliver of moon shines brightly.I twist and search the darkness for the stars of the big dipper in the north. Gran's cottage on the North shore should be right under it. Nothing but darkness in the distance. There are pin-points of light on the shore in the direction Bobby went. If the lights are Cascade, then the cottages are the other way. I try to remember how far. Can I do it? Can I swim that far? I'm not sure. I haven't swum in a lake since that awful summer I was eleven. But I did learn to swim. In high school, in a pool, with the water depths written with paint at the waterline and water never so deep that I couldn't touch the bottom with my toes while my head was above it. Rain drops fall lightly as I begin a slow crawl.

It seems an eternity, and my arms are aching when I stop to tread water for a moment. My eyes are accustomed to the darkness now, but there isn't much more than water to see. I'm searching the sky frantically for signs of the dippers when a low voice travels across the water's surface. I stop all movement for a moment and listen. I can't hear the words but the voice is coming from somewhere ahead of me. I pull myself though the water, listen, then pull myself farther. The voice is familiar. I realize when I feel the sand under my feet, that it is Fred. I can barely see him standing on the dock in front of Gran's cottage. He is alone and is talking, I suspect, to his dead father. I steady myself on the sand and strain to hear.

"She's family, Dad. You'd like her. I just don't know what to do. I mean, how can I tell her? It's been twenty years, and things are different now. But a crime was committed, Dad. A crime. I can't just ignore it. God, I'm sorry I just didn't let it go. Why did I have to dig it all up? She's good people, Dad. And she's family."

He hangs his head and slaps the piling. The water seems warm around me, but my arms and chest above the waterline are covered with goose bumps. He's talking about me. Somehow he's found evidence and he knows what I did. But how? The box is in my car and the evidence it held is long destroyed. Did I leave something on the boat? Oh, God, is this never going to end? I let my knees bend and with a gulp the water covers me. What do I do? Maybe Bobby is right, just let myself sink, all my troubles will be over. Bobby. Oh, God. Whatever happens to me, I have to tell Fred about Bobby. I have to. Billy Campion is in danger. I have to tell him. I straighten my legs and rise above the water. There are two people on the dock now, and they are arguing. I strain to hear what they are saying.

"Right!" Fred yells and they leave the dock together.

I try to call out, but it's like a rock is lodged in my throat. I cough and one of them looks back toward the lake, but they don't stop. By the time I drag myself up to the dock, I am shivering and coughing but I can finally gasp. "Damn. Shit. Hell."

25

I'd cry, but climbing out of the water took all my energy. The air raises immediate goose bumps on my arms and my wet clothes hang like ice bags on my body. But the dock is warm, the heat of the day baked into the rough boards. I close my eyes, stretch myself across it and feel the warmth against my skin. The shaking calms to a constant shiver. I'll just lay here a minute, just a minute. . . "Sweet Jesus!"

I open my eyes and see Officer Campion stumbling towards me. I try to smile but my face aches. I can't seem to raise my head. His hands are warm on my shoulders.

"Molly!" Campion shouts. "What happened? What are you doing here? Are you all right?"

With Campion's help I peel myself from the decking. I try hard to swallow. "Okay," I croak. "B. . . Billy?"

"Billy? What about Billy? He's with Carol and the girls. Look, we have to get you dry and warm. I've got a blanket in the car; I'll drive you to the hospital."

I shake my head wearily. He's already pulling me up. God, he's warm. I fall against him and he reaches under my knees and gathers my limp body in his arms.

"Fred's then," he grunts.

"No," I rasp into his neck as hot tears trickle down my cheek. I can't face Fred now. "Not Fred's"

He stands me up next to his car and covers me with a blanket before pushing me into the seat. My elbows and knees bend uneasily as he leans across me to fumble with the seat belt buckle. When he pulls back, the involuntary shaking returns. His hand on my forehead feels like ice.

"Fever," he says, looking deep into my eyes. His are so dark, with just a hint of copper at the edges. Copper? Pennies? Something I should tell him. . . . but I'm so tired. . .

I hear tires crunch on gravel and the car stops. A little fumbling and I'm being carried. A familiar jingle and the smell of chocolate brownies and brewed coffee.

"Will." Flo's voice. "What's happened?"

"Found her on the dock down on cottage row. Wet, feverish."

"Bring her back."

We follow Flo behind the counter and down a short hallway.

"Gotta use your phone," Campion says, awkwardly dropping me into a chair.

"Go," Flo tells him.

By the time Campion returns, Flo has stripped off the icy bundles masquerading as my clothes, wound my head in a large dishtowel and dressed me in soft sweat pants and a huge flannel shirt. She folds the sleeves up to my elbows and helps me hold a cup of warm broth. I'm still shivering. She pushes up one leg of the sweatpants and massages the leg. I moan softly as feeling begins to return to the muscles. Flo waves at Campion to rub the other leg.

"Where's Billy?" I whisper as he kneels beside me and carefully pushes up the pant leg.

"He's with Carol and the girls. They're worried about you."

His hands are warm and tiny electric shocks shoot through my body when he touches me. I feel oddly safe, sitting in Flo's break room, in strange clothes, being massaged. I sip the warm broth and close my eyes. "He tried to kill me," I say.

"Billy?" Flo and Campion say together.

I open my eyes and rasp. "No! Bobby. Bobby M ..
m . .Matthews tried to kill me. Well, he did. . . o or at least he
thinks he did. And he's going after Billy. You have to protect
Billy."

"Hold on, hold on." Will Campion looks relieved when he
pulls the sweat pant leg down and backs up to sit on the edge
of the only other chair in the room. I see myself reflected in
his dark coppery eyes. "Start from the beginning, Molly. What
were you doing on the dock?"

The faint jangle of bells interrupts. Flo takes the empty cup
from my hands and moves to the doorway. "You two work this
out. I got customers."

"Molly," Campion leans forward, takes my hands and
repeats. "What were you doing there?"

A wave of nausea shudders through me. I close my eyes
and try not to throw up. "I went to meet Yvonne Cooper. But
she didn't show."

"Yvonne had an accident. She's at the hospital."

"What?" My eyes spring open, making my head hurt. The
nausea's gone. "Is she all right?"

"Will be. She hit a parked car in Chandler. Would have
been fine but she had a take out coffee in her hand and it
scalded her. Think she was trying to use her cell phone. Why
were you meeting?"

"I don't know. Something about the cottage, I guess. Billy
and I were here, having ice cream, and she came in. She asked
me to meet her at the cottage later."

"Billy was with you?"

"Yeah."

"Oh. So, you went to the cottage. Then what happened?"

"Well, Bobby Matthews was there."

"And?"

"And he killed his wife!"

"How do you know that?"

"He told me, and then he pushed me in. He thinks he killed me."

"By pushing you off the dock?"

"No. Off the pontoon, in the middle of the lake."

"You willingly went out on the lake in a boat with Bobby Matthews?"

"Well, no. Not exactly. But it's hard to explain. He was telling me about his development plans and then, we were out in the middle of the lake, and he got a call, on his cell phone. I guess it was the hospital, telling him Kyle was dead.He went ballistic."

"And he told you he killed his wife?"

"Well, not at first. At first he was yelling at her. And then I guess he remembered I was there. He told me how he did it, how he killed her and then some kid came back for a shovel or something, and he killed him too."

"The Chavez kid. Should have guessed."

"Who was he?"

"Joey Chavez, a 15-year-old kid, disappeared around the same time as Charlene Matthews. Listed as a runaway. His father comes into the station from time to time. Good man. Always said his boy wouldn't run away. Damn. What does this all have to do with Billy?"

"He BLAMES him. He said it should have been Billy and not Kyle. Don't you see. He wants to kill Billy."

"It's all right. Billy is at Fred's. Matthews doesn't know that and we've got an APB out on him. He showed up at the hospital with a gun, threatening everybody. Howard Santini's pressing charges for assault. There's a warrant out for his arrest.

Road blocks here and on the state highway. It's just a matter of time. He's not going to hurt anybody else."

"Promise?" I feel hot tears creeping behind my eyes and look down while I try to will them away. If Bobby finds out I'm still alive, he might not worry about whether it looks like an accident. Suddenly I want to see Fred, and tell him everything. Campion puts his hand on my shoulder.

"Are you going to be okay?"

"Yeah. Will you take me home now?"

He helps me stand. I feel a little dizzy, but I can walk with a help. We pass slowly though the restaurant. Flo holds the door and gives me a small hug as I leave. "Take care of her," she tells Campion.

"What did you say to Yvonne?"Campion asks as he starts the car.

"What do you mean?"

"When you talked to her tonight.It must have been something to get her so upset."

"I can't think of anything I said that would upset her. Billy and I were just having ice cream."

"Maybe Billy said something."

"No, He wasn't even there when she came in. He went to the bathroom."

"Oh. What were you eating? You know, when you saw Yvonne?"

"Ice cream. I had plain vanilla and Billy had vanilla on a peanut butter cookie."

"With butterscotch sauce?"

"Yeah."

"That explains it."

"Explains what?"

"Yvonne. When I saw her at the hospital she said we were history. She accused me of seeing another woman. You actually. I guess she assumed the "Campion Special" was mine."

"Oh, I'm sorry. I could talk to her."

"No." Will Campion's eyes locked on mine. Reddish brown glints almost cover the dark iris. "It wouldn't have worked anyway. Yvonne and me. No fireworks."

He hesitates, I swear I can see tiny copper colored explosions in his iris. Then he looks away, puts the car in gear and backs out of the Shoreline parking lot. I can still see the exploding pinwheels on the back of my eyelids when I close my eyes. I let the hum of the car engine lull me to sleep.

26

"Sweet Jesus!" Will hisses and hits the brakes. He's out before I can unfasten my seat belt. "What happened? Are you all right?"

It's Carol. She's framed in the headlights, leaning over a shape on the gravel shoulder of the road, I pull myself up on the open car door and peer into the darkness. Billy and Fred's girls are standing just beyond the headlights, hugging each other and crying. There are dark stains on Carol's shirt and on the pavement. Neighbors are starting to come out of their houses. Still holding on to the car I walk around the door and lean against the fender.

"He's been hit!" Carol sobs. "On purpose!"

Oh, my god, Fred. My knees buckle and I lean heavily into the car.

"Who would want to hurt Old Sam?" Billy's voice echoes across the scene.

Not Fred? Old Sam? Memories cut across me like dull razors.

"Carol," Will says. "Did you see. . .?"

A huge bear of a man lunges into the circle of light. "Officer, Officer! Oh hey, Will. It was a black Lincoln. One of them Limo rentals, I'll bet. Went through like a bat outta hell, Damn fool. Could'a' been a kid!"

The dog whimpers and wrestles sideways. Carol pushes him down and staunches the flow of blood from a wound on his hindquarters. "Ben," Will says to the witness. "Can you take Carol and Old Sam to the vet clinic in Chandler? I'll call ahead and tell them you're coming. Billy, get a blanket for transport. Molly?" He turns in time to see me slide down the side of his car and into oblivion.

I'm aware of distant voices. A phone ringing. Then a cool hand on my forehead. Then Billy saying, "Dad, Dad she's coming around."

My head feels like a bobber, rocking on rough water. When I open my eyes, the rocking slows. I try to sit. Dizzy. Billy helps me get upright. "Dad!" he yells.

I recognize the overstuffed cushion of Carol's porch furniture. Will Campion backs through the screen door with a steaming mug and a sandwich. I smile weakly and ask. "Old Sam?"

"No news yet. Carol said she'd call. The girls went with her." He sits next to me and offers the mug. "You need to eat something." Then to Billy he says, "Find a blanket son, can't have her passing out again."

When I close my eyes the rocking returns. I open them and accept the offered mug. Hot chocolate. I take a small sip, shake my head at the sandwich. Will looks at it a moment then takes a bite. Billy returns with a crocheted afghan and helps Will arrange it over my shoulders.

"It's okay, Molly," he says between bites of sandwich. "You're safe now. But I have to go. Yvonne called dispatch, she's pretty shook up. Said Bobby Matthews came by her place. Acting odd and asking about Billy. She doesn't think she told him anything, but she took the sedative they gave her at the hospital, and she's kind of spaced. Anyhow, she's plenty scared. They sent an officer out to check her out. Now they're a man short on the search team. I have to go. You need to get inside and lock the doors."

"But you said I was safe."

The phone rings in the house and Will motions to Billy to answer it. He waits till the screen door closes behind the boy before clearing his throat and speaking in a much lower voice.

"Matthews probably thinks you're dead, but he might come here looking for Billy. If Yvonne, let something slip. I'm pretty sure she didn't, and anyhow, there's six different roadblocks between Yvonne's and here, so chances are, he's gonna get caught real soon."

"But?"

"But you can't be too careful."

"We'll be fine," I tell him. "I just want to sit here a while longer, get my bearings. We'll go in a minute. Maybe you could just turn out the light."

"Dad," Billy hollers from the house. "Dad, it's dispatch."

Will swallows the last bite of sandwich and passes Billy at the door. The yellow bug light gives Billy's face a ghostly pallor through the screen. He lingers inside, scuffing his shoes against the door.

"We got him!" Will tells me, nearly knocking Billy over as he bursts through the door. "I have to go, You'll be all right now. The state boys found his car at the Marina and got lucky. I'll be back."

As Will's cruiser backs down the drive, Billy turns out the bug light and joins me on the porch. We sit quietly in the darkness. Me in the wicker couch covered with Carol's afghan and Billy in the chair opposite, chewing his lower lip and fingering the laces of his shoes.

Wisps of grey clouds scurry across the sky, covering and uncovering stars, constantly changing the quality of the darkness. Billy's voice filters though the shadows.

"Molly?"

"I'm here, Billy."

"Kyle's dead." The wicker chair squeaks and I feel rather than see Billy cross the porch. The couch cushion exhales as he lowers himself next to me.

"I'm glad he's dead," Billy whispers. I can't think of anything to say.

"He wasn't so bad, you know. I mean, he acted like a jerk most of the time, but. . . I mean, we were friends and all. Dad said his neck was broke, real broke. Like he couldn't feel anything anymore. He'd hate being crippled, like that. Not being able to feed himself, or pee alone. He'd rather be dead than like that. You know?"

I draw the afghan tighter across my shoulders, and think about Uncle Ed drowning in the lake, Gran drowning in a bottle of whisky, myself - drowning in guilt.

"Molly?"

"What, Billy?"

"Where do you think he is now? Kyle, I mean."

"I'm sure he's still at the hospital, Billy."

"No, I don't mean his body. I mean Kyle, where is Kyle now?"

I choose my words carefully, remembering Helen's hysterical response when I asked about where Cliff went. "I think his soul is in Heaven," I say, hoping he won't ask more.

"Do you think he's with his mom, now?"

An ache blooms in my chest, completely apart from the soreness my body feels. My throat constricts and tears run unchecked down my face. "Yeah, Billy. I do."

"Me too," Billy says.

The weight of Billy's head pushes against my shoulder. I lift my arm and allow his head to fall into the hollow between my shoulder blade and neck. He shudders, slightly. I cover him with the afghan and pull him closer. Under the August night sky, two eleven-year-old souls let go of the troublesome day and fall into dreamless sleep.

27

Rain splashing on the ground and the porch roof wakes us. Cool winds and spray seep through the afghan and raise goose bumps on my arms.

"Billy?" I whisper. He groans and I squeeze his shoulders. "In the house," I tell him. "We should go inside." Wind gusts topple trash cans a few yards away and the cold rain whips in all directions, drenching the porch and the wicker couch and us. We manage to get inside as the sky opens up and crashing thunder follows the heavy drops of rain. I lean heavily against the kitchen table, feeling the percussive jolts through the soles of my feet, dripping rainwater on the linoleum. My legs are weak and I ache everywhere. "Towels," I say and Billy stumbles up the stairs in the dark to fetch some. Flo's flannel shirt is only damp but the sweat pants are soaked. I wring out the afghan, lay it across the wooden drying rack Carol uses for dishtowels and wrap one of the towels Billy brings ineffectively over the soggy sweats. He mops up water we tracked in from outside. The kitchen clock is dark. I wonder how long the power's been out. Shouldn't Campion be back by now? And Fred? Oh God. I really need to talk to Fred.

"We should go to bed," I say out loud.

With Billy's help I climb the stairs and we find the way to our rooms in the dark. I shed the sodden sweat pants and lie as gently as I can on the bed. My joints ache and my bones settle uncomfortably into the mattress. The smell of damp flannel fills my head. I close my eyes and think, rather than speak my childhood mantra. "Om, mani, padme, oooommm." The uncomfortable bed, the dark room, and even the awful ache, fades into dream.

The ribs of a row boat curl around me. Nothing but blue sky and decorative tufts of cloud are visible from the prow to the flat transom where Uncle Ed's old Evinrude motor hangs motionless. Oars, locked in their metal cuffs near my hands, rattle against the the sides of the boat. "Molly, go ahead Molly-girl, dive in, " I hear Uncle Ed say. "Go away, Go away," I beg. "She's family, Dad." It's Fred's voice saying, "It's been twenty years and things are different now, but a crime was committed. A crime." And then Bobby Matthews says, "I like you, Molly; I really do. But you can see the problem, can't you?" I hunker in the bottom of the boat, close my eyes against the mocking blue sky. "Stop it! Please. Stop!" As if to answer, something strikes the boat. I open my eyes and watch the old Evinrude tip, balance precariously for a moment, then fall backward with a splash. I raise myself cautiously to peer over the edge and watch the surface rings of water expand as the motor rides the lazy current of the lake in a downward spiral and disappears into the murk. Is it just the water, or is there something else? I peer past my rippled reflection, into the depths beneath the boat. Something circles, rising. A shining horse. No. The grille of a car with a mustang emblem on it. Bump! It hits the boat and moves slowly past, toward something else in the water. Another boat. Well, what's left of a boat. A burned out carcass, charred ribs hissing slightly as it succumbs slowly to the waves. An oar floats by. I reach instinctively and grasp at empty oar locks. Water seeps through between the planks and puddles on the boat bottom. I push myself up to the seat and watch as the water circles my ankles, rises on my legs. The boat fills and I hold the sides, as if I could lift it out of the lake by sheer will. I feel the cold water envelop me, and I sputter like a dying motor, let go of the boat and begin to kick.

I wake, shivering. My head throbs and my stiff limbs are tangled in the bedclothes, but I am safe, on dry land. In my cousin Fred's house. The clock is blinking in the darkness. The power must be back. How long have I slept? I can hear water rattling down the drainpipes and faded distant rolls of thunder. The storm has passed, for now anyway. Perched for a moment on the edge of the bed, I wish I could talk to Fred, then realize Fred and Carol are probably already sleeping, and Campion's probably bunked on Fred's couch downstairs. Everyone is sleeping. It will have to wait. It can wait. It's waited all this time; it can wait. I hope Old Sam made it. In the bathroom the night light is just enough to show me the aspirin. I shake them into my hand, two, no three. Toss them into my mouth and cup my hand for water to help them down. There are no towels; I grip the flannel shirt to dry my hands.   .

The rain has not made it cooler, only more humid. I lie down and stare at the ceiling, rub my arms, wonder if I have a fever. I close my eyes and listen to the lake play the Evers dock like a xylophone. Boats creak and rattle as small waves raise and lower them, and then it tap dances its way across the sand. It isn't silence, it's a symphony. Quieter than the raucous jam of squealing tires and heavy bass I am used to, but not silent.

A loon howls across the water. A low rumble, like distant thunder or maybe a boat motor breaks the restful rhythm. And then it is gone. The loon calls again, and then a splash and rough scraping sounds draw me to the window.

My eyes adjust quickly from the darkness of the bedroom to the slightly lighter grey of the night. Moving among the shadows I see a figure bent over a boat hauled up on the shore. I am about to call out "Fred," but as I lean forward the figure straightens, triggering the sensor light on the dock. Bobby Matthews looks up quickly into the beam, and then leaves the boat and moves out of the frame of the window.

For a moment I am caught in the surreal landscape of boat and dock; then the motion light goes off. I can't remember if I locked the doors. I peel myself away from the window, grab jeans from the chair and walk into them as I head down the hall. It's all right, I tell myself, Fred's here now.

Zipping and snapping, I push open the door to find Billy's bed empty. I back track to the bathroom. "Billy," I whisper at the door. "Billy." No answer. I push open the door. The bathroom is empty. I tell myself he must have gone down to sleep with his father on the living room couch. I hesitate before starting down the stairs. Where did Bobby go?

I'm on the bottom step when the kitchen door squalls open. I hurry down the hall to the living room, where Billy and Campion are not sleeping, look into Fred and Carol's room where the bed is undisturbed and keep going toward the street side door. My hand is on the knob when Bobby speaks.

"Well, now. You're just the person I've some to see," he announces in a voice thick with anger and booze. I lean into the door to keep from collapsing. And then I hear Billy say, "My dad told me about Kyle." Oh ,God, Billy. I make my way back down the hall toward the kitchen.

"Oh, he did, eh?" The bitterness in Bobby's voice reminds me of Uncle Ed.

"Kyle was my friend, Mr. Matthews. I wish I could have talked to him. You know, said good-bye and all."

"Really? Well, Billy, you know, you can still talk to him."

"Huh?"

"Come on outside, Billy. I'll show you what I mean."

"Okay."

"No!" I yell, stepping into the light.

"What the?" For a moment Bobby's face loses all color and he shrinks back toward the door. But he recovers quickly and pulls a small pistol from his jacket pocket. "How did you manage?" he asks, waving the pistol.

"Billy, come here," I say softly.

"No! Billy, stay right where you are; I'm not done." He aims the pistol at Billy but looks at me. " Very clever, but not clever enough. I don't know how you did it, Molly Swain, but it doesn't matter. You know what I have to do. You're only making it harder."

"You don't want to do this," I plead.

"Don't want to. No. I don't want to. But you can see, I have to. You do see, don't you? I don't have any choice here. I never have a choice. No choice. Now, let's all go outside." He motions with the pistol and Billy moves hesitantly toward the door. Bobby waves the gun for me to follow. I walk slowly, struck by the storm of emotions struggling beneath the angry redness on Bobby's face. Something about the tightly pinched nostrils and flushed cheeks is all too familiar. Uncle Ed. Uncle Ed when he found Fred and me with the dog up on Hunter's Ridge. My stomach roils as I remember the dog's thick hair matted with blood and the powerless rage that filled me. I will not let this happen again. I will not! I stop, my hands on the door jamb, Bobby pushing me from behind, Billy turning to look at me. "Run, Billy. Run!" I scream.

Billy looks back for a minute, nods at me, then sprints across the yard. By the time Bobby gets past me, Billy has disappeared into the night.

"Shouldn't have done that, Molly." Bobby pushes me roughly toward the dock.

"I couldn't let you kill him."

"Doesn't make any difference, Molly. I'll find him again, after I take care of you."

Our bodies trigger the dock light sensor, flooding the beach area with light. For a moment I mistake the rowboat pushed up on the sand as Uncle Ed's, shiver briefly with the memory of my eleven year old self. But I'm not eleven anymore. I'm not a child and I refuse to be pushed any further. I stand straight and manage to keep the little voice inside me from screaming. "I'm not getting in the boat," I say in as even a tone as I can. "You'll have to shoot me, here."

"Don't think I won't," Bobby sneers.

"Do it then." I challenge him.

He raises the pistol and aims it at my head. "I like you, Molly. I do, really. But this is who I am. I'm sorry."

"Do what you have to do," I say, my eyes closed and my body stiffened for the impact. I wonder what it will feel like. I wonder if Will Campion will come to my funeral. I wonder if Ed and Gran and the dog will be waiting for me on the other side. The other side? I open my eyes and look directly into Bobby's eyes. "When I see Kyle, I'll tell him all about his father. I'll tell him how you killed his mother. How you were going to kill his best friend. I'll tell him that when I see him. Won't he be proud?"

Tears gather at the corners of Bobby's eyes, spill over and run down his cheek. The pistol lowers slightly. "My boy," he says softly, his chin quivering. "My boy is dead."

"And it's your fault!" I whisper, louder than I intend.

"What?" he asks sharply, the pistol jerked up again. "What did you say?"

"I said it's your fault. All of this is your fault. You killed your wife, and that boy. You started this whole awful sequence of events. If you hadn't pushed that car into the lake, it wouldn't have been there for Kyle to fall on. And now your boy is dead too. It's your fault!"

He steps toward me.

If I'm going to die, I'm going out swinging! "It's like a whirlpool," I tell him. "What you did in anger ten years ago keeps coming around and it's dragging you deeper and deeper. And it's just going to keep dragging you. Believe me, I know."

"She's right Bobby." It's Fred's voice, followed by a sharp crack. I feel my throat tighten, a burning sensation. Fred is standing just outside the reach of the dock light, looking strangely at me. I put my hand on my neck and try to swallow, feel the warm blood flowing down my arm.

Bobby aims the gun at Fred who looks at me, then back at Bobby. "She's right" he yells. "You started this with Charlene. It's time to stop. What are you going to do, Bobby, kill everyone in Cascade? Everyone in Chandler? Everyone knows, Bobby. Stop it here."

"No," Bobby says, looking at me.

I want to scream "You shot me!" but only gurgling sounds come out. My knees feel weak.

"No,". Bobby says again, looking at the gun in his hand. "It wasn't Charlene."

"You killed Charlene, Bobby." Fred's voice is panicked; he's looking at me like he's seen a ghost. "You started this mess; you have to stop it!"

"No,". Bobby says again. "It was old man Stephenson."

"What are you talking about, Bobby? Grayson Stephenson was an old man, and he died years before Charlene; he couldn't have killed her. You killed her."

"I know! I killed her!" I can hear Bobby now, but I'm having trouble seeing him. "It started with old man Stephenson. He was sick. Told me he was going to sell the business, wanted me to find a buyer. Why should he sell it? What would he do with the money? He was old and sick, and I was the closest thing to family he had. He should have given the business to me."

"He did give it to you Bobby; it was in his will."

"Was it? No. No, he was old and sick, but he wasn't dying fast enough. Charlene was pregnant and wanting me to marry her, and the old man wasn't dying fast enough, so I helped him. It was easy, and writing the will was easy too; I'd been doing all his paperwork, you know. Man hadn't signed his own name in years. It was all working out too . . . then Charlene found out about it and she just couldn't keep still, and then that kid with the shovel. He saw me.I had to kill him. It wasn't so hard, you know. And then my boy. . . oh God, my boy. . ."

"Bobby, we've known each other a long time. Are you gonna kill me too? End this now, Bobby. End it." Fred's voice sounds very far away.

"Yeah," Bobby sighs. "You're right, time to end it." The crack is muffled. I fall to the ground, no longer able to hold back the blood.

Someone is squeezing my arm. Someone else is pressing on my neck. We're moving, a siren is wailing. I'm very cold.

28

No one expects me to talk. They talk, I just nod and smile. The bandage on my neck is stiff but barely shows under the swirls of my blue scarf. Old Sam sticks close to me, his own bandages more apparent. It's reassuring to stroke his head and know we're both going to make it. It hurts to swallow, though, and I haven't tested my voice yet. When I need to say something, it's in a breathy whisper. The doctors said my vocal cords were badly bruised, but not irrevocably damaged. It's the swelling, they assure me, that's causing the problem. Actually it's kind of a reprieve. One good thing about not being able to talk is I don't have to return Helen's calls. When Fred brought me my cell phone, there were 35 unanswered calls and four messages, all from Helen. Whatever Helen wants, it can wait till I can talk again. Another good thing is I can't tell Fred how I killed Uncle Ed. Oh, I am going to tell him. Maybe the authorities will have pity on my eleven-year-old self, but regardless I can't let it drag me under anymore. Right now, though, it's nice just to relax and listen to him recount our more recent adventure.

"Well, he wasn't in his right mind," Fred says to the young reporter from the Tribune. Carol, standing behind him, only clears her throat, doesn't correct him. "It's nearly ten years since his wife disappeared, you know. And finding her drowned right here in the lake was a shock. And then his boy's death really unhinged him. You know, sent him over the edge. Molly was trying to talk him out of killing himself when I got there. I don't think he meant to shoot her, the gun just went off in the excitement of the moment and Molly was there. And then, when he saw what he'd done, well, I think that was the last straw. He, uh, he pointed the gun under his chin and it was over."

"What about the roadblocks and the all-points bulletin? Weren't the police involved?"

"Well, that's true," Fred tells the reporter. "Howard Santini, the hospital administrator, notified the police after Mr. Matthews had a mental breakdown at the hospital. Concern for Mr. Matthews' safety prompted the roadblocks. The APB was just to inform law enforcement to be on the lookout."

"That how it was?" the reporter turns to Will Campion, who looks very official in his dress uniform.

"Pretty much," Will says clearly. " The individual was known to be armed and potentially violent. The department is charged with protecting its citizens, even from themselves. The general public was never in any danger."

"Well," the reporter looked smug. "Miss Swain might disagree with that."

"Miss Swain is clearly an extraordinary individual," Campion replies, looking directly at me. "The department commends her for her courage and willingness to help her fellow citizens. Now, if you'll excuse us, we're on our way to a funeral now."

It's a good story. Sort of glosses over the fact that Bobby Matthews killed three people, ran over the Evers dog and tried to kill me, twice! When I can talk I'll have to ask Fred about that.

It's been a busy day for the graveyard staff. Three white tents are erected in the small cemetery. Two, only steps apart in the older section where Fred's father, Uncle Ed, and Gran are all buried. The third is set at an angle, in the newest section, where a white pickup truck full of flowers is parked.

The cemetery is much the same as I remember it. Not a lot of crying, though. None at all for Bobby Matthews. I guess most of the tears have already been shed for Charlene. And there's no one left to cry for Kyle. Fred helps me out of the car, but it is Billy Campion who takes my arm as we walk toward the first tent. Carol and Fred take seats in the front row. It's a small gathering, only three rows of folding chairs. I sit in the third row, with Billy on one side and Fred's girls on the other. This is the first time I've seen the girls in dresses. I swallow uncomfortably, looking down at their patent leather shoes. The past comes to haunt me again. Granny Evers scowling at my worn sandals and Helen shrugging her shoulders in resigned acceptance.

I look up and see Yvonne Cooper seated in front of me. Her bandaged hand nervously brushes away the no-see-ums that have begun to gather. Her pale fingers and freshly painted nails stick out from the gauze wrapping and look like large matches. I expect them to burst into flame any moment. Next to her, dapper in his thinly striped suit, Harold Santini sits erect and solemn.

Odd that I should remember him now. It was a hot summer afternoon a long time ago. Helen and Cliff had taken a walk, and left me reading a book and dangling my feet at the end of the dock. Harold had left the gaggle of kids playing a sort of beach ball tag a few cabins down and swum under the Evers dock. He came up between the dock and the rowboat smiling and asked, "What'cha readin'?" It was My Antonia, I suddenly recall,

The funeral director reads from a small black book, his voice nearly monotone, the words almost unintelligible. "Ashes to ashes, dust to dust . . . " I watch him reach into a small box near the podium, and toss the handful of sand on top of the casket. He nods to Fred and walks across the grass toward the other tent. Fred and Carol rise together and each takes a handful of sand from the box. Fred lets the grains fall thoughtfully through his fingers onto the casket top. Carol opens her hand, letting it all drop at once and then quickly brushes any remaining grains from her palms. The girls follow their parents as Harold and Yvonne step toward the grave. I swallow hard, try to clear my throat. I wonder if I should have stayed in the hospital another day. I'm not sure why I'm here. Billy taps my arm and together we walk around the back of the chairs and follow Fred and his family.

There are already mourners in this tent, and flowers. Two caskets lie on a single bier, red roses atop one, a small bouquet of daisies on the other. They are surrounded by arrangements of lilies and glads and chrysanthemums. A vase of long-stemmed roses sits on the podium where the minister presides, his voice at once solemn and comforting. After the sermon he invites those with memories to share to come forward. Carol begins, telling about the time she and Charlene hitchhiked to Petoskey and got their ears pierced, then she takes two roses from the vase and places one on each casket. Fred and some of the other mourners share stories, place roses and return to their seats. When Billy takes his turn, he stands facing the caskets and says simply, "Kyle was my friend. I miss him." Instead of taking a rose, Billy tugs a small piece of blue paper from his pocket, unfolds it and slides it under the daisy bouquet. The minister leads us in a moment of silent prayer and it's over.

It isn't Billy that takes my arm this time; it is his father. "Folks," he says softly as he guides me between the chairs. "Could you all follow us please? Just down this way." Whether they know where they are going or are compelled by his authority, the entire group of mourners follow us across the grass to the third white tent and the pick-up full of flowers. After the small service Joe Chavez Sr. nods his head and thanks each person personally, for remembering his boy.

29

As we stand at the gates of the cemetery, Carol whispers in my ear. "Molly, there's a sort of pot luck over at the Shoreline. Do you think you're up to it? We have to go back to the house for my salad. And then we're going to walk down to the diner."

I nod. I've been eating Jell-O for a week; actual food would be a welcome change.

"I'll drive Miss Swain over," Will Campion says. "Don't want to wear her out, do we? Have you seen Billy?"

"Over there," Carol says as she points toward the road where Fred and Billy and the girls are standing. "He's actually talking to the girls, Will. Why don't we meet you two at the Shoreline? We'll take Billy with us."

"Sure. Okay with you, Miss Swain?"

I nod and smile weakly. I wish he'd quit calling me Miss Swain, He guides me to his pick-up truck with a gentle hand on my elbow. The bandage tape rustles when I scratch at at it.

"I hope you don't mind, I have something I gotta do, it's on the way, won't take a minute"

I nod and he puts the truck in gear. His hand on the seat back grazes my shoulder as he looks through the back window before backing up. Then he turns back, changes gears and pulls out into the road. We pass the Shoreline Diner, where cars from the cemetery are beginning to arrive, and take Crooked Lake road toward Cascade. When Campion stops the truck on the shoulder behind the old cottage, I'm surprised by how calm I feel. The smell of the pines, the vibrations of the truck left running, and the warm breezes spilling gently through the truck window envelop me. I close my eyes, lay my head back against the headrest and breathe in. The past week, even the past 20 years peel away like the thin skins of dry onion and float out the window with the air. I feel at once exposed and surprisingly whole.

The clunk of Campion's toolbox against the truck bed nudges me back to reality.

"You okay?" he asks, climbing into the cab and putting the truck in gear.

"I'm fine," I whisper, and think to myself that it's true.

He stops at the corner, waits for a car with it's blinker on to begin turning before he pulls wide into the intersection and makes a u-turn. As we pass the cottage again, I ask. "What'll happen to these cottages now?"

"Don't know, exactly. Got a lot of paperwork to sort out. Seems Matthews put Yvonne's name on a lot it, trying to cover his tracks, I guess. She'll probably have to act as some kind of executor for the partnership."

"What about the other partners?"

"Weren't any."

"Oh."

"You sign anything yet?"

"On the cottage? No. No I haven't signed anything."

"Well then, it's still yours, Miss Swain." he says

"Molly, please call me Molly." I croak.

"Molly, then."

"What about the others?"

"Well, the ones that have actually been paid for would most likely be probated. Or, more likely go to bankruptcy. I don't know. Might not be too complicated - I mean legally that is. Matthews had no relatives that I know of, and I doubt any are likely to come out of the woodwork now."

I have to clear my throat and swallow, then say softly, "You've given this some thought."

"Yeah. I have. Yvonne told me that 'North Shore Development' was more or less a front.   Now that I think on it, I wouldn't be surprised if the actual sales were never closed on. I wonder if the sellers would still sell. If they went cheap, I wouldn't mind buying one or two of them myself. Hell, I'd buy them all if I could. Works of art, every one of them. You still want to sell, Molly?"

I shrug and then ask, "What would you do with them?"

"Hadn't thought that far."

"You could rent them, you know like a resort," I hear myself say.

"Like North Shore? No way. Might as well set 'em on fire and whip up a good wind."

"Aquarius," I correct him. "He was going to call it Aquarius, after the constellation."

"He tell you that? I guess you two were pretty close." His knuckles tighten on the steering wheel.

I swallow hard. The ache in my throat tightens and tears gather in my eyes. "He tried to kill me," I rasp, my fingers tracing the bandage on my neck and then rearranging the folds of blue scarf. "Twice."

"I'm sorry. Really, I, I didn't mean that like it sounded."

He looks ahead, seeming to concentrate on the traffic, but working his jaw like he's holding back a flood. We ride silently to the Diner. The gravel lot is already full and a few cars have parked on the shoulder. We pull up behind Joe Chavez's pickup, just a short walk from the diner. Before he shuts off the engine, Will looks at me as if he has made a decision, and I am again aware of the metallic flecks in his dark eyes.

"Molly," he says, putting his hand over mine on the car seat. "Before we go in, I got to tell you how sorry I am. It's my fault you got hurt."

I shake my head, but he keeps talking.

"I shouldn't have left you alone that night. But the state boys were sure they had Mathews cornered at the marina. I should have left it to them, but I wanted to see him caught. Stupid. It's my fault that he got to you. Took us nearly an hour to clear the scene and see he'd got away. When I got back to Fred's, they were loading a body into an ambulance and I was afraid it was you. I, um. I lost my wife, you know, couple of years back. It was a bad time. When Laurie died, I just lost it. I blamed myself for everything. For not being there. For the pregnancy and her death. I coped by walling myself off from everyone. Maybe even from Billy. Oh, I went through all the motions, you know, did what was expected. But I wasn't really present - if you get what I mean."

Oh, I think I do. I nod.

"Then Fred told me it was Matthews. He said you had been rushed to emergency. By the time Billy and I got to the hospital, you were in surgery."

"It's okay."

"No, listen. Well, when I got to Fred's that night, and Billy came running at me, he was screaming that you'd been shot, I. . . Well, it's like a big crack just burst in that wall and all that pain and all those memories came flooding back. And when Fred told me how you saved Billy, risked your own life for his, I just, I just. Molly, I'm so sorry."

I'm swallowing hard again, and my throat is tightening. "Let's go in," I whisper.

Flo is busily directing a buffet of casseroles and deserts laid out on two long tables near the cash register. Carol waves at us from a booth near the back and Campion moves us through the crowded aisle toward her. "Saved it for you," Carol says as soon as we're seated. "You stay here and I'll get you a plate. Will, you want to help me?" They are gone before I can protest.

I'm watching them pick and chose among the dishes as they fill two plates. Carol begins to spoon something onto the plate, Will stops her and puts his hand to his neck, making a squeezing motion, and Carol puts the spoon back. Yvonne slips into the seat opposite me, slides a dish of fruit with the palm of her bandaged hand onto the table top and carefully places a mug down with the other. She taps the side of her cup erratically, then rubs the rim with her middle finger. Finally she speaks.

"Can you ever forgive me?"

"For what?" I whisper.

"For telling him I was meeting you at the cottage!" she whispers frantically back. She lowers her head and grasps the cup firmly with her good hand. "I had no idea he'd do that, you have to believe me."

"It's okay," I tell her. I see tears gathering at the corners of her eyes and put my hand over hers on the cup. She is actually shaking. "Really, Yvonne, it's not your fault. You couldn't know. You couldn't."

"Oh, God. I just didn't want you to think that I would do anything like that, on purpose I mean. So, we can still be friends?" She looks up hopefully.

"Of course, we're friends," I whisper. And I mean it. There's no reason Yvonne and I can't be friends. My throat is aching. I take a pen out of my purse and write on the back of a napkin, What did you want to talk to me about, at the cottage that night, anyway?

"Well." She turns the napkin over, picks at the gauze near her thumb and says,"It was so obvious, I don't know why I didn't see it before. I was going through the escrow papers and reconciling the North Shore account and I realized it was just paper."

Paper? I write on the napkin.

"Yeah. You see, Bobby created North Shore Development before he came to me, and I thought it was going to be just a straight commission on sales deal on the properties. I didn't know very much about the corporation. But Bobby said if he made me a partner, I would make a lot more money. So he had me sign a few papers, but he did all the work. Anyway, whenever I had a question, he would put me off to later and make me feel silly for asking. He was good at that. Anyway, after the accident, with Kyle in the hospital and all, he hadn't been even opening the mail for the development. Well, I hated to bother him, you know, so I was trying to do the accounting work myself."

I nod.

"Yeah, and the thing is, North Shore wasn't funded." She pops a grape into her mouth and waits for me to answer.

I write a question mark on the napkin.

"Well, that's the point, don't you see? All the paperwork was there for all the properties North Shore was buying, but there wasn't any money so none of the sales were going to close. I'm afraid the offer he made on your property isn't any good. I'm sorry."

I write Not going to sell on the edge of the napkin and slide it to Yvonne.

"What's that?" Carol slides a plate and some flatware in front of me. Campion sits next to me with his plate and Carol slides in beside Yvonne.

Yvonne shows Carol the napkin.

"That's terrific, Molly," Carol says. "What about the rest of Cottage Row? I mean, I guess Bobby's resort won't be going through."

Everyone looks at Yvonne, who quickly swallows the piece of fruit she has been chewing. "Well, I'm not sure. Nothing has apparently been filed with the county and none of the properties have legally changed hands. I was just telling Molly, North Shore Development wasn't funded, so I guess it's all back to square one. I expect I'll have to write to the owners and apologize."

"You mean, Matthew's plans were all hot air? Figures. Where was he going to get the money? Those 'investors' that screwed up the lock? How many properties are we talking about, Yvonne?" Will asks.

Yvonne looks at him for a moment as if deciding something then says, "Well, there are eight cottages next to Molly's. Then there's 6 lots, some of them very small, on the canal and some acreage behind that."

I quickly snatch Carol's napkin and scribble. Do all the owners want to sell?

They all look at me, and Yvonne says, "I guess so; I mean, they think they already have."

"Well, what if someone," Will looks at me and continues, "or several someones wanted to buy them?"

"Well, I guess I could write new offers and just go on as if the original offers didn't exist." She pulls at a wisp of gauze on the palm of her bandage, then looks up and says, "Which I guess is actually true."

I look down at the plate of food in front of me. Jell-O. Orange Jell-O. I pick up my spoon and try to remember how much discretionary money I have in the Trust. The Jell-O slides cooly down my throat. It would be like any other investment, wouldn't it? Next to the Jell-O some kind of fluffy mixture of fruit and marshmallow. I have to chew it, slowly. It's very sweet. Cliff, if you're listening I hope you approve. I move on to the macaroni salad. It's harder to get down but I chew very deliberately and close my eyes to swallow.

30

Everyone is out on the lawn. We're having a picnic. Voices mix unintelligibly with the sweet blur of dog barking and childish laughter. I had the lawyers overnight me the latest statements on the trust and the numbers look pretty good.

"Hey, cousin, looks like you're feeling better."

"Yeh," I breathe. I look up at Fred and smile.

"Got a minute? I um, I need to talk to you."

"Sure," I whisper, and Fred sits down. "I have something to tell you too."

"You've been through a lot, cousin. Hope you won't hold it against us."

"Not your fault," I rasp, stroking the bandage on my neck. "What was that fairy tale your told the news guy?"

"No point in prosecuting a dead man, Molly. Besides, I'm saving the taxpayers money. All the evidence is here say. There is no actual evidence that Bobby killed Charlene, or old man Stephenson, either. No fingerprints, no witness, no nothing. With a good lawyer he might even have gotten off."

"But he did it. He confessed. You heard him."

"Here say, Molly."

"Well, what about the Chavez boy?"

"I talked to Joe. He doesn't want reporters following him around. He's a good man. Says we can't bring the dead back, and the living got to keep on living. Smart man, Joe Chavez."

"Yeah," I say.

"Hey, Molly, remember when we were kids and you and the professor used to walk around the lake?"

"I remember."

"Did you know I was walking behind you most of the time? Not following you exactly - just wanting to be a part of it."

"No, I never knew," I whisper and then cough to clear my throat.

"Cliff did. He used to leave money with Flo, for an ice cream with sprinkles for me. She always said it was 'on the house' but a couple of years ago she told me."

"Sounds like Cliff." I push the paperwork forward on the table and lean back in the chair.

"Remember that last summer you and Helen came up, and I put the spider in those damn hot dogs and we all came here for dinner. It was a plastic spider, by the way. Gran hated spiders so much she just freaked when she saw it and never touched it. Threw the whole pan out, hot dogs and all! Remember that? That was the night Uncle Ed did the fireworks out on the lake"

I swallow hard before I answer. "You mean the night he died?"

"Yeah. I've been wanting to talk to you about that. It wasn't an accident, you know."

"I know."

"What do you mean, you know? How?"

"It's what I wanted to tell you. It was my fault." I hold my throat, and wheeze out my confession. "I drained the engine so he'd get stranded out on the lake."

"Why'd you do that?"

"To get back at him. Childish anger. He took me out in the boat and threw me in a couple of days before. Said I should learn to swim. I damn near drowned." The strain on my throat makes me swallow hard several times. Then I continue. "He killed the dog. Remember? I wanted him to feel what I felt. I didn't mean to kill him. But it all went bad. It was all my fault." The effort drains me. I close my eyes and try to swallow the ache in my throat.

"God, Molly I'm so sorry, I had no idea. But you didn't kill him. Really."

"Hmmm?"

"It always bothered me, you know, how hush-hush everything was after he died. I've been sort of investigating it since, like, high school. It was actually Bobby that solved it for me."

"How?"

"You know," Fred hangs his head and sighs. "I've known Bobby Matthews almost my whole life, and yet., I didn't really know him at all. Old Doc Andersen came out of retirement to do the autopsy for me. I just couldn't, you know. Turns out Bobby was addicted to oxycodone, among other things. And of course he drank. He was a bomb waiting to explode. Made me remember something about Uncle Ed that I'd forgotten."

"I don't understand." I pull at the bandage where it is chafing my neck.

"Uncle Ed was taking a whole cocktail of pain killers when he died, Molly. Mind bending, mood altering medications to counteract combat fatigue. They call it post traumatic stress disorder now. But it messes with the mind something awful. Uncle Ed killed himself, Molly. Went out with a case of beer and fireworks. Had a grand old time flinging the rockets into the air. Then he set the boat on fire and shot himself with a flare gun."

"I don't understand," I repeat. "No one ever . . . How do you know? "

"It was hushed up. I got Andersen to talk about it after he finished with Bobby. He knew that the insurance wouldn't pay Gran if it was a suicide. So it had to be an accident. On paper, anyway. He said he figured it was the war that really killed Ed anyway, and so Gran was entitled to his insurance. Helen confirmed it. She suspected something wasn't right, just couldn't put her finger on it. Oh yeah, Helen called the house while you were in the hospital. She was worried because she couldn't reach you on your cell. I told her you accidentally dropped it in the lake. Told her you'd call her later. She said it was really important."

"Uncle Ed killed himself?" I lean back in my chair and let my hands fall to my lap.

"What? Oh, yeah, but you're the only one I'm telling. Water over the bridge and all that. Some secrets should remain secrets."

"Why tell me?"

"Well, that's why you never came back here, right. Bad memories? I was hoping if you knew, you might stay awhile. You're welcome at our place as long as you want. Carol, and some other folks I know, would really like you to stay too. What'a ya think?"

"Well." I take a deep breath, look over Fred toward the door. Billy Campion is showing his dad how to turn the handle on the ice cream bucket. "I'm thinking about fixing up the cottage, to live in, full time. I might be able to invest in a couple of the other cottages and generate some kind of income."

Fred smiles broadly. I touch my bandage lightly and whisper, "I have to stay until the doctor says this is okay anyway. Think you could get me some of that ice cream?"

"Sure," Fred starts to get up. "Speaking of ice cream, the paper that young Campion left on Kyle Matthews casket. Seems it was a gift certificate for ice cream. Mackinaw Island Fudge. Any idea what that's all about?"

"Nope." I say and Fred leaves to help the Campions with the ice cream.

Some secrets should remain secrets.

AFTERWARD

"Last one in's a rotten egg!" Fred hollers, charging out the back door and across the lawn. The screen door slaps closed and the three children chase Fred toward the water. Freddie passes her father and hits the water full gallop.

Billy told me he's decided that Freddie's pretty cool, for a girl. She's promised to show him a place on the big lake where turtles lay out on downed trees to sun themselves. He'll have to help row, but he says he doesn't mind.

Fred catches up, and for a minute he and Freddie play water-slap at each other, laughing and ducking from the spray. Billy looks back at Charlie, who's already slowing. She's got short little legs and I think she's always the egg. Billy exaggerates a stumble and goes down. Charlie passes him, and running as fast as she can. Billy gets up slowly, smiling, and is running again when she hits the water. She turns and smiles big, before falling stiff backed into the waves. Good for you, Billy. I watch as he runs as far as he can into the lake, and when the water is too strong, he lets his knees buckle and falls in. When he stands up and catches his breath, Charlie is splashing him with water-slaps. He looks back at the Evers porch where his father and I are sitting on the wicker sofa and waves. I smile, remembering this is his first swim in the lake since the accident. and wave back. Carol backs out of the kitchen door with a pitcher of lemonade and a stack of tumblers. Will rises to help her.

I've hired Will to help me fix up the cottage. He's planning on running for Sheriff next year but says that Billy is a crack

hand with a hammer and plenty old enough to pick up the
slack. He'll be twelve next Thursday. Will's planning a
birthday party at the Shoreline. Even Yvonne is coming.

Billy helps Charlie climb onto a large tube and drags her
thru the water. Their laughter is contagious but my throat aches
with a sudden urge to cry. A rash of chilly goosebumps rises on
my arms. Twenty years ago, Uncle Ed pushed me into that
water, and I vowed my revenge. Twenty years. All those years I
remained a frightened eleven-year-old, alone with my deep,
dark secret. Helen, awash in her own anguish, unable to help
me. I shiver and unconsciously reach for my throat. Will takes
my hand, and squeezes it. The shivering subsides.

When the swimmers return to the house, wrapped in beach
towels, their wet hair plastered to their heads, I see that the
scar on Billy's forehead is already fading. I wonder about the
wounds we cannot see. The shards of memories, etched deeply
in his psyche. The sooner this summer's traumas are forgotten,
the better. The sharp edges of my own memories here are
dulling. Perhaps I'm healing.

Billy's a good kid. For his sake, I hope they've got Mackinac
Island Fudge Ice Cream in Heaven.

ABOUT THE AUTHOR

Ruth Hankins is an Artist, and Author, who lives with her husband in the north woods near Grayling, Michigan. As a Graphic Designer her projects ranged from simple logo designs to hot air balloons and stained glass patterns, lottery games and corporate advertising campaigns. Retirement has given Ruth the creative freedom to exhibit and sell her artwork (including ceramics, textiles, jewelry, painting and poetry) in the AuSable Artisan Gallery in Grayling. She is able to share her love of art and poetry by teaching classes and participating in local open mic events. Crooked Lake is one of three novels she has written with a midwestern, small town setting and character driven story lines.

Made in the USA
Charleston, SC
08 October 2013